MALL YOU NEED IS LOVE

AT THE MALL HOLIDAY STANDALONE NOVELLA

SARAH ROBINSON

CHAPTER ONE

AMARA

*W*HY AM *I not even surprised?* Amara Hart scrunched up her nose as she stared at her ex-boyfriend's Tinder profile on her iPhone screen. She'd just been swiping to pass the time during her shift at work when she'd come across him, and now she found herself reading his bio with disgust.

Aaron, 34: Looking for someone who can be discrete. DM for digits.

She closed out of Tinder and opened Instagram, checking to make sure she hadn't completely lost her mind when she thought she'd seen he'd gotten married recently. Sure enough, when she got to his profile feed, there were tons of photos of him and a cute blonde wearing a giant engagement ring on their honeymoon. They'd literally gotten married last week, and he was already back on Tinder? Hell, it was Valentine's Day this weekend!

Once a cheater, always a cheater. Man, she'd really dodged that bullet.

Not that she really considered Aaron to be much of an outlier, though. After Aaron—and a slew of other short-term relationships that had all ended in heartbreak and disappointment—Amara had committed to staying single for the foreseeable future. Hell, maybe forever. Relationships were for people who were willing to settle for mediocre, and love was a Hallmark scam meant to pad the pockets of corporate bigwigs who preyed on lonely people on a commercialized holiday. Bah humbug, or whatever the Valentine's Day version of that was.

At thirty-two years old, Amara knew she still had a lot of life left to live, though she couldn't help but feel like the dating years were behind her. Good riddance.

"Frogger is on the fritz," Jean announced as she walked up to where Amara was standing, leaning against the cash-out counter. "Can you fix it again?"

The young teenager was leaving for college in the fall and Amara wasn't sure what she was going to do without her. When Amara had first opened Rad Retro Arcade three years ago on the west end of Yule Heights Shopping Mall, she hadn't expected her small town in Michigan to respond so well to a room full of original video game consoles and tables. She had everything from Pac-Man to Donkey Kong and she valued her little business as a place to step back in time and leave all her current woes at the door, and thanks to being pleasantly single, she didn't have any woes to worry about right now.

"Did you unplug it and then plug it back in?" Amara asked. That was always her first question, and half the time, it did solve the problem.

Jean rolled her big blue eyes. "Yes. Twice. I think you have to do a system reset."

"All right, all right," Amara agreed, heading over to find the Frogger machine by the SkeeBall ramps lining the back wall, currently packed with four different groups of teenagers all cheering one another on. She smiled at them, glad to see them here having fun with one another in person instead of on their cell phones ignoring the world from separate rooms. One of her regulars sank a high score ball, and she offered him a thumbs-up. "Good shot, Marco!"

"Thanks, Mara!" the young boy called back, using her nickname. "Hey, can we get some cheese fries?"

"Sure, kid." She had already asked the kitchen to prep an order when she'd seen them come in. Marco didn't often have enough money to play the games and order food, so usually he did one or the other. Sometimes she liked to make sure he was able to do both, so she'd send him some free fries from the restaurant down the hall. While she didn't have a kitchen of her own, she had worked out a partnership with The Big Cheese food truck parked in the courtyard, along with eight other food trucks that served all the mall patrons. They provided her customers with a small discount on food, and she let them use her storage room after-hours for supplies.

After a few minutes of fiddling with the Frogger gaming system, she got it up and working again but had lost the last week of high scores data people had been accumulating. She frowned, hating when things like that happened, but thankful that it was only a week's worth. She glanced over at the Ms. Pac-Man game a few rows down, praying that never happened to her high score record there. In fact, she'd once been Michigan's highest scorer for the entire game and she'd been working on making a national title for herself before the championship league had been shut down for lack of funding...and interest.

Story of her life.

"It's working again," Mara told Jean as she returned to the counter. "Can you go check on the last two orders at The Big Cheese? They should be ready for pick up."

Jean nodded, then pointed toward the receiver for the landline against the wall. "Yeah, but you just missed a call from the charmer next door. Don't worry, I got him to call his dogs off."

Mara internally groaned. "Let me guess, he said the kids were being too loud and disturbing his fancy, rich customers?"

She laughed, nodding her head. "I mean, not in those exact words, but I think that sums it up pretty well."

"Go get the cheese fries." Amara ushered her off, chuckling. Complaints from the neighbors weren't entirely uncommon, especially when she'd first opened and had stolen half the mall's customer base, who now spent hours in her arcade instead of purchasing trinkets from other mall vendors. But these days, the complaints all seemed to be coming from one place—Kisses and Karats Jewelry. She didn't know the store owner well, except for the rumors circulating around the other shop owners at the mall that he was a ladies' man. In fact, the owner of Tequila Mockingbird on the south end swore he'd broken her heart when he didn't returned her text messages after a date. One of the hairdressers at Barber Streisand said he saw him making out in the parking lot with the wife of the owner of Son of a Bun Bakery. All that to say, she had no interest in getting to know the reckless Casanova, nor was she interested in keeping her store quieter so that he could sell more diamonds to misguided saps who had too much money and not enough imagination.

Her luck was short-lasting as the entire arcade suddenly went dark.

"What the hell?" Amara stood up straighter, trying to adjust her eyes to the sudden blackout.

"Hey, what's going on? The game turned off!" A kid from one end of the arcade complained loudly.

"Sorry, folks. The power will be back on in a minute," Amara announced, quickly making her way to the back room to find the circuit breaker. The rest of the mall still looked completely illuminated; only her store had gone off. What the heck was happening? She'd never had an outage in here before.

When she arrived at the circuit breaker, it took all her might to pry the metal panel apart, and when it released, it flew open so hard that it hit the wall behind it with a clang. She had never had to look in here before, and none of the switches in front of her were labeled as to where they went as she held her cell phone's flashlight up to the box. She examined it for a few seconds before deciding to just flip all of them and hope for the best.

Thankfully, that seemed to do the trick.

The back room lit up with the familiar fluorescent glare, and Amara sighed at the stack of video games that had toppled over against one wall. She went to pile them back up, not even sure why they'd been left here in the first place, when she realized the back door was ajar. Every store in the mall was connected by a small, dingy corridor that ran the length of the mall and allowed store owners to take out trash or receive shipments without walking it past the customers through the front door. Aside from the nightly trash run, she always kept the door locked, because the retro games she carried at her arcade were expensive, and she wasn't willing to see one of them walk off and end up on eBay for a collector to snatch up.

Amara pulled the door firmly closed, ensuring the bolt settled into place. She turned the lock, frowning as she made a mental note to remind Jean to be more careful when coming and going. As she returned to the floor, she passed out extra tokens as a courtesy to the customers who'd lost their gaming streaks with the outage, and everyone was appeased and happily playing again within minutes.

Jean walked in with a large tray full of cheese fries and other cheesy items. "Who ordered these again?"

Amara handed her the order slip with the names and locations of the customers. "Hey, did you leave the back door open earlier? All the power went out in here."

"Really?" Jean's brows lifted. "No, I haven't used the back door today."

"It was definitely weird, but I was able to get it back on pretty quickly," she confirmed. "But yeah, just make sure you keep that door locked."

The rest of the shift went by with no incident until Jean was putting on her jacket and getting ready to clock out. "Uh...Amara?"

"What?" She turned to look at the young girl, then followed her gaze to the three police officers walking through the front entrance of the arcade. "Uh oh."

"Should I stay?" Jean asked.

"Did you commit a crime?" Amara joked. "No, go on home. I'll talk to them. I'm sure it's just a complaint from *Kisses and Karats* again."

Jean rolled her eyes and gave a small chuckle before clocking out on the payroll app on her phone and then waving goodbye.

"Can I help you folks?" Amara asked as the police officers reached the counter where she was standing.

A tall man with a thick mustache tipped his hat to her. "Ma'am, we're here about the incident next door."

"Okay, we told him that we'd try to be quieter, but we can't control our customers. They're not being rambunctious or disorderly or anything. They are just playing." Amara waved her hand toward the room, indicating her gaming customers. "He didn't need to call the police on us."

A female officer standing to the mustachioed man's right frowned. "No, ma'am. This is about the robbery earlier today. We need to ask you a few questions."

What? "Wait...there was a robbery?" Amara's mind immediately went to the open back door, and she quickly scanned the arcade, trying to see if she could spot anything missing. Her stomach sank at the idea of having to make a report to insurance. Her rates were already insanely high, and this was just going to skyrocket them. "What was taken?"

"Not here, ma'am," the woman continued. "Next door. Over fifty thousand dollars' worth of jewelry was stolen from the back room at Kisses and Karats earlier today. Were you not aware of that?"

Her eyes went wide. "No! That's terrible. Is everyone okay?"

Despite her feelings toward her obstinate neighbor, she would never wish something like that on any small business owner.

The officer pulled out a notepad and a pen. "No one was injured, but we'd like to see any security footage you have from today, as well as anything suspicious you might have witnessed."

"Oh, uhm...I don't actually have any security cameras in here. The mall does in the main hallways, so, you know, I figured why double up on that expense?" Heat rose to her face, and she wondered if her explanation sounded as stupid out loud as it did in her head. In trying to minimize her monthly expenses, that hadn't seemed like the most important thing to focus on, but now she was second-guessing that decision. "I did find the back door unlocked earlier, though. That was strange. It's never unlocked or left open, and my employee said she hadn't used it all day. Nothing was missing from our back room." She frowned. "I guess I *could* double check more thoroughly."

"Why don't you go do that," the officer agreed. "Officer Powell will come with you and we'll take a look around, if that's okay."

"Sure, help yourself." She gestured to the store floor. "Just don't try to beat my Ms. Pac Man record."

Her joke fell flat as the hairy-lipped officer frowned at her. "We're working, ma'am."

"Right, uh...okay, well, this way." Amara headed toward the back room as the female police officer followed close behind. The room was pretty small, and not exactly the picture of organization, but it was pretty easy to see that everything that was supposed to be there was there. "Nothing seems to be missing."

"What happened there?" Officer Powell pointed to the circuit breaker that she'd left open to remind herself to test each switch later and label them.

"Oh, the power went off earlier. I guess the fuse box blew, but I flipped the switches, and it came back on pretty quickly. I just need to label them, because that's never happened before."

"The power went off?" The officer's brows raised, and she pulled out her notepad and a pen. "What time was this?"

Of course, that was something that they would have wanted to know about. She couldn't believe she hadn't already mentioned that. "Uh, around one o'clock, I guess? Lunch time, for sure. But it was very quick."

"I'm going to need you to write a statement about all of

this." Officer Powell handed her a form. "Do you have a pen, or do you need one?"

"I have one," Amara said, grabbing one off the back table. "Uh, sure. I'll just fill this out now."

The officer stood stoically and watched as she began writing.

She didn't have much to say, but she repeated the information she'd given the officers and then included her contact information before handing the form back to her. "Here you go."

"The store owner next door would like to talk with you as well," the officer commented as they headed out of the back office.

Great. She secretly groaned but gave a tight-lipped smile. "Sure thing."

Dealing with the Hallmark playboy was the last thing she wanted to do today.

"Mr. Rossi?" A female police officer walked through the front entrance of Kisses and Karats Jewelry store with a shorter woman tailing behind her.

He looked up from his laptop, which was sitting out on the glass display case as he worked on filing a claim with insurance for today's robbery. Valentino Rossi had been the owner of this franchise location for six years, and never once had there been a break-in until today—three days before his biggest money-making day of the year, Valentine's Day.

"Any news?" he asked the officer. "Insurance says I need a case number from you guys."

Officer Powell handed him a document with the information he needed. "We're still conducting interviews of potential witnesses. This is Amara Hart, owner of Rad Retro Arcade next door."

Val's eyes lifted to the woman standing slightly behind Officer Powell. He hadn't paid much attention to her before. The name was super familiar given how many times he'd called over there and asked her to keep the noise to a minimum, but not once had he actually met her in person, and she was nothing like who he'd pictured.

Not that he'd really spent much time picturing her at all, but the woman in front of him was wearing a sleeveless sheath dress that stopped right above her knees and a flannel sweater was tied around her waist. She wore black and white sneakers, and her hair was multiple shades of pink, purple, and red streaking through platinum white, falling across her shoulders and down her back just enough to partially obstruct the colorful tattoos covering the upper half of one of her arms.

"Amara Hart?" he asked again, then stepped out from behind the counter and extended a hand. "Uh, well, it's nice to finally meet you in person."

"Is it?" She cocked her head to the side, a sly smile pulling at her lips.

She didn't bother to take his hand, and he dropped it after an awkward moment. "Well, I'm sure you heard about what happened earlier today. The robbery and all that."

"Yeah, I'm sorry to hear about that, but I'm not sure how I can be of much help," she replied. Despite the fact that she was at least a full foot shorter than him, she stood with so much power that he found himself stepping back slightly. "We're not missing anything over at the arcade, and aside from the power outage, everything has been pretty routine today."

"The power went out?" His attention caught on that detail, and he turned to look at the officer. "Did we know this? Could that have turned off the security system at the back door?"

"That's the current operating theory," the officer confirmed. "We think whoever broke in did so first to the arcade to shut off the power, and then easily made it inside after that was disabled."

"Was your security system not on?" Valentino returned his gaze to the arcade owner who looked like a deer in headlights. He crossed his arms over his chest, the sleeves of his thick burgundy sweater pushed up on his forearms. Thanks to spending four days a week at the gym, he was proud of the muscles clearly prominent in his arms...and everywhere else. It gave him a formidable look that made him unapproachable to some and even more enticing to others. But he wasn't focused on that right now, because this woman had cost him a lot of business over the last year, and if she'd also been partially responsible for him losing almost his entire inventory, he might actually blow a gasket.

"Uh, we don't have a security system. But there's a lock on the back door. I have the key right here." She held up a key hanging at the end of a lanyard around her neck. "We've never had an issue before this. This is a really safe area."

"That's all it takes though, Ms. Hart. One time, one slip up, one break-in, and we lose everything." He shook his head. He couldn't even believe he was having this conversation right now. "It's beyond me how you don't have a security system. I thought the mall required that in our leases. How can you run a business like that?"

"Hey, guy, I'm not the one who got robbed, okay?" Amara perched her hands on her hips and glared at him. She looked taller when she stood like that, and her cheeks flushed pink, which normally he would have found really cute if she wasn't being so gosh dang aggravating right now. "Nothing in my lease says I'm required to do anything other than lock the back door—which it was. It always is."

"Obviously, it *wasn't*." He gritted his teeth and went back to his computer behind the counter to finish his insurance claim. "I need your information for the insurance claim as well, since they used you for access."

Amara sighed, but there was clearly a look of guilt flashing across her face. "We don't *know* that they used the arcade, but the back door was open earlier today. I had the key the entire time, though, and my employee didn't even go in the back room today."

"So, it wasn't locked." He threw up his hands in frustration, then looked back at the officer who was only half paying attention as she wrote in her notepad. "Did the lock look like it was broken? Like someone had tried to pick it or jimmy it or something?"

"Two officers are examining it now, and that will be included in our report. But listen, folks, in these types of situations it's best not to point fingers and try and find blame. The only people to blame are the criminals. I would recommend putting in a security system, though, ma'am. Until then, maybe the store owners can form a neighborhood watch of sorts?"

"Neighborhood watch? For what?" Amara frowned, looking up from the paper she was writing her information on for him on the glass display case top. Val tapped the paper, urging her to get back to finishing writing. "You think they'll be back?"

Officer Powell nodded. "In all likelihood. Where there is one break-in, more usually follow. They got a good amount of inventory, but they didn't get everything. They might consider doubling back for the rest or hitting the arcade next. I saw you had a Frogger machine in there. Those things can sell for a pretty penny in an online auction, and now that they know they can get in through the back door, they might be coming back with a truck to transport. They hit a jewelry store in the middle of the day, so I'd say these criminals are probably more ballsy than we think. Either that or stupid and willing to take the risk."

"What?" Amara looked alarmed and her voice went up at least two octaves. "Are you serious?"

"That's why business owners pay for security systems," Val reminded her, as if that wasn't what he'd been saying this entire time. "These doors could be popped open with a credit card or one good kick."

Her face paled, her fingers fidgeting with the pen in her hands. "Well, maybe we *should* do a neighborhood watch thing."

"I'll be the first to sign up," Val replied, because there was zero chance he'd be able to go home and sleep easily tonight. The idea that maybe the robbers could be back to finish the job was way too much of a risk that he couldn't afford right now. He only had enough inventory to cover current orders for Valentine's Day, and if he lost that, the entire month would be in the red. Insurance would probably help reimburse the lost merchandise to a point, but likely not at full value or taking into consideration all the customers he'd have to turn away until he was fully stocked again.

"Me, too," Amara agreed.

"Great," Officer Powell responded. "Well, why don't the two of you take tonight and we can arrange for other store owners to start setting up a schedule."

"Tonight?" Val glanced toward Amara, not exactly looking forward to spending his off time with her. "I mean, I can do it alone. You don't have to be there."

"Oh, so your store is protected, and my arcade gets robbed?" Her hands were on her hips, her elbows jutting out as she looked at him with irritation. "I don't think so. I'll be there."

"Fine." He shrugged as if he couldn't care less. Which he really couldn't. Except, why was he feeling a stir of excitement in his gut? He pushed away the intrusive thought, but it was persistent. Was he eager to spend a few hours alone with her? Absolutely not. The idea didn't even make sense. There was literally nothing about this woman that was even remotely in common with him. "When does the arcade close?"

"Ten o'clock." Amara pushed her hair back behind her shoulder, then handed him the piece of paper with her contact information. "You can call or text when you're ready."

"Great. I can't wait." He took the paper from her and scanned her handwriting—did she seriously dot the letter *i* with a heart? "Oh, and you should probably tell your boyfriend or whatever you'll be spending the night here. You know, in case someone needs to know where you are."

She frowned and her eyes narrowed into small slits. "I don't have to report my whereabouts to anyone, thank you very much. No one is going to be looking for me."

Val found himself smiling, lifting one brow to stare back at her. "That's an odd thing to be proud of."

"I-I didn't m-mean it like that," she stuttered, her eyes going from small slits to wide open. Her normally hazel-colored skin turned darker on her cheeks, and the tip of her nose even seemed effected. It was actually kind of endearing, and he found a warm feeling filling his chest as he watched her try to spin her way out of her statement. "I meant it like I'm my own boss. I own the entire arcade, you know. I don't report to anyone."

"Congratulations," he replied, purposely pushing her buttons now.

"I don't even have a boyfriend," she continued, definitely

in some sort of word vomit ramble at this point. "Not that I couldn't have one if I wanted. I could have a boyfriend. I have had boyfriends."

He smirked at her again. "Good to know."

She didn't bother trying to respond, but this time just let out an irritated huff then turned and stormed away.

"Wow. I would not want to be you tonight," Officer Powell said, turning to look at him over her notebook.

Val shrugged. "We'll be fine. We're the best of friends, as you can tell."

"Right." Officer Powell pursed her lips, non-chagrined. "Well, here's your report. Sign the bottom for me and you can keep the copy. We'll be in touch as soon as we find something."

"Thanks." He handed her back the paper after he'd scrawled his name across the signature line and torn off the copy. "Have a good Valentine's Day, by the way. We'll have a sale going if you're looking for any jewelry for your partner."

The officer didn't respond to him but took the paper and left. Val stood at the counter for another moment, contemplating his next move—both today and in life. This store had always been his dream after watching his parents run a local jewelry store in his youth. When they both passed away in a sudden car accident in his early twenties, he'd been forced to close their store to pay off the debts they'd accrued. He'd vowed to himself that when everything was paid off, he'd build the store back up again, this time under his watch. It wasn't that he didn't respect how his parents had done things, but they'd struggled with the business side of things. They'd been so into the craft and the artwork of matching the perfect piece of silver or gold with a person or a story or an event...that they'd let the rest overwhelm them. Val was determined to do the opposite and build a lucrative business in memory of them both.

And yet, he'd just taken a financial hit that all could have been avoided with smarter business choices. More security. Less inventory on site. He was angry at himself for letting this situation occur, and he was even angrier at whatever dumb criminals had ruined his entire week—hell, month, year—in their rash attempt at grabbing his riches.

Val looked around the empty storefront with the gate pulled down in front. It was closed—obviously—but he had at least four more hours to kill before the arcade closed and their watch patrol began. Neighborhood watch with Amara Hart? Definitely not at all how he'd seen his shift ending today. He heaved a sigh and went to the back office to brew himself a cup of coffee so he could stay awake. Might as well keep working on all the insurance forms, since he didn't have anything better to do.

At least not until later tonight.

Why did that thought send a rush of energy up his spine?

CHAPTER THREE

AMARA

WELL, that had been humiliating.

Amara stormed back into the arcade after her word vomit session in front of her neighbor. Had she seriously just told him that she was hopelessly single a few days before Valentine's Day and that no one loved her enough to care if she went missing? That wasn't true, obviously, but why the hell had it come out like that? She groaned as she went back behind the counter and located her cell phone, pulling up her best friend's name.

"Hello?" Nell answered the phone after just one ring.

Amara let out a sigh. "Please tell me again why I don't want a date on Valentine's Day."

"Because you insist on being straight, and men are absolute garbage," Nell responded without so much as a pause. The two women had met over a decade ago at a gaming tournament and, despite coming from pretty different backgrounds, they'd hit it off immediately. Amara was the youngest of two girls in a loving family and her parents were still together after almost forty years in a small lake cabin upstate. Nell was a former foster kid who had found her chosen family through a foster brother and his new wife and children. Even since they'd moved out to Silicon Valley when he'd gotten successful in the app world, though, Nell had been lonely here in Michigan, and so she and Amara had been spending more time together than ever before.

She laughed, the tension in her chest already easing. "I mean, after Aaron...I could probably be convinced to join you in the lesbian web."

Now it was Nell's turn to laugh since she was the one who had first told Amara about the joking concept of all local lesbians being somehow connected romantically to one another through some degree of separation. "It's an open invitation anytime. What's got you in your feels today?"

"I'm spending the night with the man who owns the jewelry store next to mine," she replied, this time leaning forward on the counter to support herself on her elbows. "And I just told him that I'm single and no one loves me."

"Wait...what?" Nell's voice almost squawked through the phone. "Rewind, because I feel like I missed ninety percent of this story."

Amara filled her friend in on the details of the recent break-in and her awkward verbal exchange with Valentino Rossi. Explaining it all over again out loud only solidified to herself how incredibly awkward her foot-in-mouth situation had really been.

"I'm not going to lie to you, Mara, that's pretty terrible." Nell was clearly holding back laughter on the other end of the line. "I mean, I'm getting second-hand embarrassment just hearing this story. Also, why don't you have a security system?"

Amara groaned. "Okay, clearly I'll be calling around first thing tomorrow morning to get estimates."

"Yeah, I'm with him on that one, Mara," Nell agreed

with her next-door nemesis. "You need security, and then more security on top of that. Do you want me to come join you two tonight on your patrol?"

She almost said yes, but she knew Nell had to be at work in the morning and wasn't about to make her schedule be upended as well. "No. It's fine. It's one night. I'm sure it won't be that bad."

"Well, I'll keep my phone on anyway, in case you want to talk at two o'clock in the morning about your new crush," her friend teased.

"That is *not* helpful, Nell," Amara shot back. They finished chatting about the latest goings-on in both of their lives before Amara returned to her job of actually manning the arcade. A few orders of cheese fries later, and one MacGyver-type repair on the Galaga shooting game, Amara was finally closing up shop, making the final announcement over the speakers that this was everyone's last chance to cash in their tokens before she closed the arcade.

"Hey, Ms. Mara, I almost made it to a thousand today," Marco announced as he walked up to the counter with his shirt scooped forward to hold the weight of the dozens of tokens he'd earned throughout the day.

"Wow." She cleared off the counter so that he could dump his shirt out. "How long were you here today?"

"Since this morning. Thanks for the cheese fries, by the way." Marco leaned against the counter and watched as she began counting out all his tokens. He pointed up at the wall behind her that had the list of prizes and pictures of what people could win. He pointed at the top prize. "I'm going to win that Nintendo Switch one day."

"It's basically got your name on it," she agreed, because if anyone was going to finally get the grand prize, it would be

Marco. The kid was short for his age, and she'd heard his friends tease him about that, but he was persistent when he was working toward a goal. He reminded her a little of herself at that age, but Marco seemed to be carrying a heaviness with him at all times that she couldn't relate to. "How's your mom lately?"

He shuffled his feet, looking down and anywhere else but at her. "Didn't get to see her last weekend. Lockdown or something."

She frowned, knowing how much Marco valued his weekend visits during family hours at Michigan Heights Corrections with his mother, who was serving a two-year prison sentence for drug-related charges. In the meantime, Marco was in the care of his twenty-three-year-old brother, who was now his legal guardian. "I'm sorry to hear that. Do you and your brother need anything?"

Marco shook his head, then dropped the vulnerable look and swiped on a sly grin. "Just that Nintendo Switch if you're willing."

"Someday soon," she promised, finishing counting his tokens and ringing his points into the register. "You're so close to twenty-thousand points on your account. You'll be there in no time."

"How many am I at now?" He leaned forward across the counter to try and see her computer screen.

She angled it so that he could see better. "Eighteen thousand, four hundred, eighty-seven points."

"Tomorrow, I'm going to hit it." Marco put both his hands up, as if to cheer himself. "Just you watch, Mara. It's as good as mine."

Amara laughed and shook her head. "I won't be here tomorrow, but I'll see you Saturday?"

"Valentine's Day?" Marco scoffed, a sly smile crossing

his lips. "How do you know I don't have a date? Or is that you asking me to be your Valentine, Ms. Mara?"

"I think thirteen might be a little below my dating range, kiddo," she joked, appreciating the compliment. "But yes, we are open on Valentine's Day—normal hours."

"Dang, you're not even closing up early? Ms. Mara, you got to get a life outside of this arcade." Marco shook his head with all the wisdom of his thirteen years on this planet. "You gotta open your heart to love, you know. There's a big banner on the store next door that says just that."

Amara laughed, because she'd seen the tacky marketing banner at Kisses and Karats over the last few weeks, trying to convince desperate couples that if they loved each other, they'd show it with silver and gold baubles. The way to her heart had nothing to do with trinkets, but, hell, beat her high score on Ms. Pac-Man and she might consider that a viable challenger for her heart. "Thanks for the tip, kid. I'll keep that in mind."

"If your dating advice is coming from a preteen, it might explain why you're still single."

Amara looked up from the register to see Valentino Rossi standing in front of her where Marco had just been. His arms were crossed over his chest, a small smirk on his lips. She'd be lying if she said she didn't notice the way his biceps didn't seem to fit easily into his sweater sleeves, or the gruff dark shadow on his chin from his beard regrowth. He must have just shaved clean this morning, and yet, it was already visibly growing back. The thought crossed her mind of what it would feel like against her skin—that prickly stubble scraping back and forth as his mouth covered hers...

Wait, what the heck am I even thinking about right now? Okay, clearly she had been single a little too long if she was lusting over her career nemesis.

"I'm not going to answer that," she replied haughtily. "I need to finish the count for tonight, but you're welcome to start patrol without me."

"It's not like we're walking around in soldier costumes," he replied, fingering one of the comic books for sale on the shelf to the right. He picked it up and flipped through it. "I can wait for you to be done. I figure we'll just pass the time and do a walk around every fifteen minutes or so."

"Why can't we alternate patrols?" she asked, not looking forward to playing the sidekick to his superhero ego. "We'll cover more ground in less time if we split up."

"Have you watched even one murder mystery movie, Ms. Hart? Splitting up is how every main character dies," Valentino replied, turning the page in the comic. "Plus, what would you even do if you came up on a burglar alone?"

She scoffed. "I'll have you know that I've been taking tae kwon do lessons since I was a kid. And you can call me Mara—everyone does."

"Tae kwon do?" He looked up at her, his gaze spanning the length of her body in a way that made her shiver with a tingle of excitement. "Yeah, that tracks. I can see that. Most people call me Val, by the way."

She wasn't sure if that was a compliment or not, but she decided not to let it bristle her. "I'm also a champion retro arcade gamer and still hold the Eastern States Championship title for Ms. Pac-Man. I think I could handle a dumb burglar who tries to rob the same place twice."

Val placed the comic back on the rack neatly and put his hands up in mock defense. "Wow, I didn't know I was talking to a celebrity. You should put that in your Tinder bio."

Amara knit her eyebrows. "How do you know I'm on Tinder?"

Now it was her turn to watch his cheeks darken, which was really saying something, since his thick scruff covered most of the lower half of his face. "I didn't...I mean, that's not...it's hard not to see your profile when I'm swiping, given how close the proximity is between us."

"So, *you're* on Tinder?" She smiled, enjoying feeling like she actually had the upper hand in their interactions for once. "I'm surprised the fancy jewelry store, Yule Heights Casanova is single right before Valentine's Day. Isn't this supposed to be your biggest time of the year to flaunt love and happiness to all the sad, lonely single people?"

"Well, you know what they say," his voice turned into a humorous lilt, and he smiled in that suave way he always did. "If at first you don't succeed, try, try again."

She rolled her eyes. "Uh huh, and how often did you try, try again with Tia at *Tequila Mockingbird?*"

Val frowned. "Tia? How did you hear about that?"

"All of Yule Heights heard about that. Over a text message? Really?" Amara shook her head. "Really, Val?"

"Hey, I'm more than happy to tell you about my side of that story," he tried to explain. "But it's probably not at all what you've heard on the grapevine. She asked me out—repeatedly. How many times can a guy say no without being labeled the asshole for rejecting her?"

Okay, so that wasn't the story she'd heard. "You rejected her?"

"Three times in person, and then at least half a dozen more times via text. Not even sure how she got my phone number." Val sighed and shook his head. "Doesn't matter, really."

"Oh. Well, I'm sorry that happened," she replied, unsure how to respond any differently. She'd only met Tia a handful of times, and while she seemed nice enough, she probably didn't know enough about her to take her word as fact just because. "But that still doesn't answer the question...why are you single on Valentine's Day?"

"Hey, I have a few days left to turn that around," he joked. "But how about this? I'll tell you if you beat me at Space Invaders."

Amara was surprised he even knew the name of one of her most popular arcade games from the late 1970's. "You play Space Invaders?"

"I did as a kid. It's probably just like riding a bike. Unless you're worried the jewelry store owner might show you up in your own arcade?" He posed his last statement as a challenge, and Amara was never one to back down from those.

She put the inventory books away and locked the register. "Never going to happen, Valentino Rossi. But I'll take you up on your wager. Let's make things more interesting though."

"How's that?" he asked.

"If I win, you tell me the real story of what happened between you and the wife at Son of a Bun Bakery—plus, why you're still single. And if you win, I'll..." She paused as she tried to think of something equitable.

"You'll agree to go on a date this Valentine's Day," he finished for her.

Amara scoffed. "A date? With who? You?"

Val laughed and shook his head. "I didn't say that. Just a date. Pick anyone. Just promise to be open to celebrating the holiday of love."

She wanted to vomit at the very thought. "Gross. But fine. You're on. We should do a quick round of patrol before I beat you, though."

"Smart," he agreed. "Except you're not going to beat me."

Together they took a quick walk around both of their

stores, the main mall hallway, the back rooms, and the back hallways before feeling comfortable with the fact that everything was securely locked, and no one was trying to break in. Twenty minutes after that and they were both neck-and-neck with their scores on neighboring Space Invaders machines.

"Okay, I'll admit," Amara looked over at him as they reached the next level, letting out a long breath. "You're better than I thought you'd be at this."

Val grinned. "See? Not just a...what did you call me? Yule Heights Casanova?"

"The jury is still out on that one," she teased. "Come on. Next round makes coffees."

Just as she turned back to the machine to begin the next level, a loud alarm sound made her jump.

"The alarm from my store is going off!" Val shouted over the piercing sound. "We need to go...now!"

"Uh..." Theoretically, she knew the answer to that was yes, but also that was the very last thing she wanted to do. She swallowed hard and tried to mask her nerves. "Okay. I'm right behind you."

CHAPTER FOUR

VALENTINO

"A raccoon? Really?" Val had both hands down by his side, a feeling of defeat sinking into his chest.

"Well, look at it this way," Amara replied, pushing the cardboard boxes that had fallen over in the back hallway of the mall and tripped the alarm out of the way with her foot. "It could have been a burglar. I think we got off lucky."

He couldn't argue with that, but that still left them with a potentially rabid raccoon that had somehow made its way inside despite heavy steel doors and multiple locks. Or maybe it had some sort of nest already inside? Did raccoons have nests? Val had no idea, and he certainly didn't want to find out. "We have to get it out of here. Hand me that broom."

She glanced to her left where a broom and dustpan were leaning against the concrete wall outside of the back door to his store. "Are you going to sweep it away? I'm not sure that's the best plan."

He took the broom from her as she handed it to him, a smile on her face as if she was enjoying every moment of his misery. "If you have a better idea, Mara, I'd love to hear it.

Otherwise, grab that long-handled dustpan and let's try to herd it toward the exit door."

Surprisingly, she did as he asked and gripped the long handle of the dustpan tightly in her fists. "Okay, but what if it...what if it, like, comes at me?"

Val shrugged. "Hit it with the dustpan? I don't know. It can't do much. It's a raccoon."

"Raccoons have killed people before, thank you very much," she huffed in response.

"What? Since when?" He began shooing the animal away from the both of them with loud, sweeping motions of the broom. It didn't budge an inch. He moved again, coming from the right side this time. Still, the raccoon kept eating whatever was in its paws like it didn't give two shakes about their attempt to evict him from the back hallway.

"I don't know—rabies? Scratching people's eyes out, sepsis from a bite wound," Amara followed suit, doing the same with the dustpan in the opposite direction so as to push it toward the exit. The raccoon just continued to stare at them like it had no idea what they were trying to do. "They are scrappy!"

Val inched closer to the animal and pushed it lightly with the tip of the broom. It reared up on back legs and stared him dead in the eyes and...hissed? A loud snarling, hissing, screeching sound came from the animal as it lunged toward him. He jumped backward so fast that he didn't see Amara had been standing partially behind him and was now completely knocked off balance.

"Ah!" Amara shrieked as they both went down in a tangle of limbs and brooms and screaming raccoons. "It's touching me! It's on me! The raccoon is on me!"

"What?" Val batted at whatever was in front of his face, trying to course correct, but all that did was land him on his back on the concrete ground. He tried to scramble back up to his feet, but the raccoon leaped directly over Amara's legs and ran down the hallway screeching like a banshee. "Mara, the raccoon!"

"It's touching me!" Mara was still shrieking and swinging her arms wildly from where she was crouched on the ground—her eyes were tightly squeezed shut and she was slapping the end of the broom away from her—it's dirty, dusty bristles on her face as it was haphazardly propped up between her and a cardboard box against the wall. "It's attacking me!"

Val grabbed the broom handle and yanked it away from her. "Mara, that's the broom bristles that were touching you. Not the raccoon. It's long gone down the hall. We lost it."

She opened her eyes and sat up straight, blinking rapidly. "Oh. Well...it could have been the raccoon."

"Except it was a broom, but okay, Lara Croft." He tried not to laugh, but the smile was certainly evident on his face. He reached a hand down to help her stand up, and she took it somewhat reluctantly. As she pulled herself up, though, she lost her footing when her heel slid on a piece of trash and she squeezed his hand tighter, only to pull him down with her.

"What the—" Val felt the wind being knocked out of him as he pitched forward, twisted in an attempt to catch himself, and landed directly on his back yanking Amara down on top of him.

"Ooof!" She landed across his chest with a loud gasp, her face inches from his. "Sorry, uh. I didn't mean to. I think I slipped on something."

"Mara, you can't just fall for me like this," he joked, but the way her eyes dipped down to his lips when he said that made his core tighten and his stomach flipflop. His attempt at levity fell flat immediately as her bright eyes found his again. God, she was really very beautiful...not that he hadn't already known that. But there was something about her being up this close that felt like more...it was the way she smelled like soft lavender and the way her hand was pressed against his chest, just hard enough that he was pretty sure she could feel his heart beating. And was it beating faster? It felt like it was pounding so hard it was going to break his rib cage open.

All she had done was look at his lips and his brain was suddenly hazy...what the heck was happening?

Her cheeks tinged pink again, and she quickly looked away with her signature eye roll before sliding off his chest. She pushed herself up to her feet and didn't bother offering him a hand to do the same, which was probably for the best, given how that debacle had just played out.

"Ha ha. Very funny," she said.

"We should, uh..." Val cleared his throat and got back to his feet finally. "We should probably do another patrol around. It's been a while. Gotta stay on top of things. Could be more raccoons out there, you know."

"Yeah, but then I've got some work to do in between patrols. I can't believe it's already almost midnight." She held up her cell phone, showing a display of 11:54pm, before she pushed it back into her back pocket. "I'm going to need another coffee."

"Same," he agreed.

They made their way back to the store and brewed their own separate traveler mugs of coffee—extra sugar and cream in hers and his completely black. He kind of liked the idea that this tough girl persona actually poured on the sweetness pretty thick, but he kept his thoughts to himself. After they were properly caffeinated, they made the rounds again to check all the locks and doors were secure.

"I've got to go run an errand at *The Big Cheese*—do you want to join me or stay here and guard the stores?" There was a slight smirk on her face as she said that, as if she didn't think he would be much of a guard without her.

"I think I can hold down the fort just fine," he assured her, but then curiosity wrestled its way into his mind. "Wait...what are you doing at the food truck?"

"Come on." She ushered him to follow her with one hand. "I could use the help carrying everything anyway."

He frowned, even more confused, but followed her anyway. When they arrived at the outdoor food courtyard, it was pitch dark with only a few security lights on around the perimeter to show the way. Amara didn't seem to have any hesitation, however, and marched right up to the large yellow food truck with a fake giant wedge of cheddar propped on the roof. She pulled a small ring of keys out of her pocket and shuffled them around in her hands for a moment until she found the one she was looking for and stuck it in the lock on the rear door of the truck.

"Voila," she said, giving a flourish with her hand as the door flung open. "Welcome to Cheese Heaven."

Val laughed and followed her as they climbed up the rickety metal stairs into the back of the truck. Everything was closed and covered, packed away for the night, but the generator was still running, keeping the refrigerated section working. He could still smell the fresh bread and cheese scent of today's preparations, and it was making his stomach growl.

"Why are we here?" he finally asked. "How do you even have a key to this?"

"The owners of The Big Cheese let me use their refrigerator overnight. They usually set out everything I need to prep, so it's super easy." Amara opened the fridge and started pulling out a stack of cheese slices, bread, and condiments. She then pulled out a large metal container of what looked to be scrambled eggs, and a plate of bacon. "Here. Place these out on the counter."

He took the containers from her and arranged them in a line of the counter. Everything was pre-cooked and looked good enough to eat—heck, he just might need a midnight snack. "Are we making sandwiches?"

"Yes, but not for us." She handed him a stack of brown paper lunch bags. "Okay, take two pieces of bread and load it with eggs, cheese, and bacon. Wrap it in the parchment paper and then put it in the brown lunch bag."

"I can't even have one?" he joked, beginning the sandwich preparations as she had described.

She just grinned at him and shook her head, then began placing apples and bananas that she'd pulled out from a refrigerated compartment beneath the counter into each bag. He added the sandwiches to the bags as they both kept working, and once she'd packed about twenty bags with fruit, she switched to placing a stack of thick, long hash browns in baggies and tucking those into the bags next.

They worked in silence for about twenty more minutes until all the bags were packed with breakfast items and stacked on a long tray.

She then pushed that tray back into the refrigerator unit and closed the door. "Okay, around five o'clock, we'll come back and grab these. The kids will probably start dropping by around five thirty, so we want to be ready for them."

"These are for kids?" he asked, following her out of the truck as she locked up everything behind them. "Which kids?"

Amara shoved the keys in her pocket and headed back toward the entrance to the indoor part of the mall as they set out to do their next patrol around the area. "Last year, the local school system ran out of funding for the breakfast program for kids from low-income families. The school still provides them a warm lunch—which is great and better than nothing—but some of these kids don't get anything to eat in a day but that. It's hard to do well in school and concentrate on an empty stomach, so some of the local businesses partner together to hand out bagged breakfasts to kids who need them. It's a great business write off for The Big Cheese, and since half my customer base—or more—is kids, I want to make sure they're well provided for if I can."

"Wow." Val hadn't heard about these efforts before, and he felt a bit out of the loop that he had never thought to give back to the local community in that way. Heck, he didn't really give back at all. There was something about the way he grew up and losing his parents that made him feel like he had to hold on to things—tight. Like if he were to let go and let people in, it would mean losing everything he owned, and everyone he loved. Because, in reality, that was exactly what had happened to his parents. "That's really wonderful that you guys do that."

She shrugged. "It's not much. I'm pretty blessed to come from a stable, happy family. My parents have been in love longer than most, and they always told us to pay it forward when we can. This is one small way I can do that."

"I think I have the opposite approach sometimes," he admitted as they walked up to his jewelry store. He surveyed the entrance, all decked out in glitz and gold. "I think I'm afraid to give things away. I'm afraid I'll never get it back. That's one of the downsides of jewelry, you know. You put all this work and effort into crafting something beautiful, and the moment it leaves the store, it loses almost all its value."

"Why do you do it then?" Her voice was soft, not judgmental, and she looked at him with a hint of concern that made him feel seen in a way he hadn't before.

"I'm not sure," he admitted. "It's what my parents did. I wanted to make their legacy successful—something they didn't manage to do in their time here. But they're gone, and that's kind of like losing all value just like these diamonds, isn't it?"

He fell quiet, and she reached out a hand to his. She squeezed his fingers gently and leaned into his side just enough to let him pretend she was holding him, or hugging him, or that the warmth of her skin was soothing the ache he was trying to push away.

"I don't know if I agree with that," she replied, her voice still more gentle than he'd ever heard it before. "People aren't things or objects to attach any sort of value or price point to. We're all just the combined essence of everyone who's ever touched us, or everyone we've ever touched, throughout our lives. That impact doesn't fade with time, or with death. It grows stronger."

He liked that sentiment. He looked over at her, angling his body toward her just enough that their hands continued to touch. He let his fingers run the length of her hand, then wrist, and up her arm until he reached her elbow. Her breath hitched, and she seemed to still beneath him. "You're not the person I thought you were, Mara Hart."

Her eyes searched his for a moment too long, making his insides squeeze with excitement and the urge to pull her against him and kiss her right then and there. But then it was gone in a flash, the expression masked by a teasing smile and lighthearted shove of her hand against his chest.

"The jury is still out on you, Casanova," she kidded. "Come on. Let's do another round before I beat you in Space Invaders again."

Valentino laughed as he followed her inside the arcade, but he felt like they'd missed a pivotal moment just then, though he couldn't identify what he might have been hoping to come from it. What was he hoping for from her?

Nothing. They were neighbors, colleagues, and...security patrol co-workers. And that was it.

CHAPTER FIVE

AMARA

"Were you sleeping?" Nell's voice came through the other line of the phone as Amara held it up to her ear and tried to register enough words for a proper greeting.

"Trying," she replied, rolling back over into the comfort of her blankets and pillows that she wrapped around herself like a cocoon every night. "I worked all night."

"At the arcade?" Nell sounded confused. "I thought it closed at ten o'clock."

"It did." Amara yawned and blinked her eyes open, trying to force herself to be alert. "But I had to do that neighborhood watch thing with Val, remember?"

"Val? You mean Valentino Rossi—the hottie next door?" Her friend was laying it on thick for first thing in the morning. Or afternoon. Or whatever the heck time it was right now. "Ooh, when are you going to see him again? Did anything happen? Is Valentino going to be your Valentine?"

Amara groaned and briefly considered hanging up the phone and just going back to sleep.

Nell laughed at her own pun. "See what I did there?"

"Yes, smart ass." She gave up on sleeping in any longer

and sat up in bed, glancing at her phone to check the time. It was almost four o'clock in the afternoon. "Yikes, I slept all day."

"I was about to say. But, hey, want to grab dinner? Or, I guess, breakfast? We should go to the diner. Best of both worlds at that place."

A cheesy breakfast burrito from Whiner Diner actually sounded really good right about now. "I'm in," Amara agreed. "Let me just get dressed, and I'll meet you there in like...an hour?"

"Make it thirty minutes," Nell replied. "I'm famished!"

Amara's front doorbell rang, and she frowned, not expecting any visitors. "Are you here now?" she asked Nell.

"What? No?"

"Someone rang the doorbell," Amara explained, climbing out of bed to go investigate. She peered through the peephole in her front door and saw a huge bouquet of flowers. "Uh, I've got to go. See you in an hour, Nell."

"Thirty—"

Amara hung up before her friend could finish that sentence, then opened the front door. "Hello?"

A delivery man in a red collared shirt held out a vase to her with a bouquet of wildflowers in dozens of colors. "You've got a delivery, ma'am. I just need you to sign here."

"Who's it from?" Not that she wasn't grateful, but she'd literally never received a flower delivery before except from her parents on her birthday and her graduation.

The delivery man grinned and gave her an awkward wink. "Read the card. I bet you'll know."

She pulled out the small white card from the middle of the flowers and opened it.

. . .

THANKS FOR AN AMAZING NIGHT TOGETHER. Here's to many more nights on the floor of the back hallway.

Happy early Valentine's Day, Valentino Rossy

"UH, this is not what is sounds like," she immediately tried to backtrack to the delivery man, though she could already feel her face on fire.

"I'm paid to mind my own business, ma'am. Just sign here." He smiled again, holding out a clipboard and pen to her.

She signed as fast as humanly possible, took the flowers and note, and went back inside and shut the door behind her with a firm twist of the lock. What the actual hell? Just when she thought maybe Val wasn't the Casanova douchebag she'd pegged him as, he sent her a card like this? One that clearly the delivery man had read and gotten all sorts of thoughts in his head about. She placed the flowers on the counter and stormed into her room to change into something that wasn't pajamas. Still fuming at his audacity, she shoved the note he'd sent in the pocket of her jeans and grabbed her car keys.

Ten minutes later, she was pulling up to the mall and finding a parking spot before stomping through the entrance and down the main corridor until she got to Kisses and Karats. Sure enough, Val was behind the counter holding up a piece of jewelry to an older gentleman with a cane standing across from him.

"Ruth is going to love this one, Harold," Val told the man, and as Amara got closer, she could see that he was holding a diamond ring on a display mannequin hand. "What do you think?"

"Val, can I have a moment?" Amara requested through gritted teeth.

Both Val and Harold looked up at her, seemingly startled at her sudden entrance.

Val nodded. "Let me just finish up with Harold, then I'm all yours."

"Actually, miss, can I ask you a favor?" Harold was turning toward her now, maneuvering with his cane to position himself in front of her. "You're about the same size as my Ruth. Can you try this on and tell me if it fits?"

"Uh..." She didn't have a prepared answer for that. "I guess so. Sure."

Harold took the ring from Val and went to hand it to her, but then stopped. "Wait, I got to do this right."

With a loud groan, Harold began to lower himself down onto one knee.

"Oh, hey, buddy." Val quickly stepped around the counter, holding a small ring pillow in his hand. He placed it on the ground where Harold's knee was aiming, then hooked one hand under his armpit. "Let me help you there, old man."

"This one's always watching out for me," Harold kidded, but with Val's assistance he successfully got down on one knee. He had one hand on his cane, keeping his balance, and the other hand extended toward Amara with the diamond ring. "Ruth Lillian Marie Alexandra McRoberts, ever since I first laid eyes on you at the Minute Clinic when we were both in line to get our flu shots, I said to myself... that's the girl for me. I'm going to grow old with her. And while I may have already been seventy-five when we met, you make me feel like I'm twenty-nine again. Ruthie baby, do me the biggest favor of my life and marry me."

"Wow, Harold." Amara was a bit taken aback by the

entire thing, but there was clearly only one answer. "Absolutely I'll marry you."

"Really?" The old man's face lit up and he slipped the ring on her finger. Val helped him get back up to his feet and she looked down at the new ring adorning her finger. It really was beautiful, and she had no doubt that whoever Ruth was, she'd love it to.

It was weird to see it there on her ring finger and not feel completely horrified. While her parents had always shown her an amazing example of what marriage could look like, her own dating experiences had certainly soured her to the idea of any sort of long-term commitment and inevitable heartbreak. What her parents had was a beautiful fluke, but it was just that—a fluke. After all the bad dates she'd been on and times she'd put her whole heart on the line only to have it crushed, she wasn't sure that was ever something in the cards for her.

But the longing in her heart when she saw this ring on her finger made her wonder if she hadn't been lying to herself. Did she want commitment? Did she want marriage and romance and all the little trinkets and tokens that came along with it? Everything about her personality would have said no, and yet...it felt so warm against her skin.

Val slipped it off her finger just as quickly and popped it back in the box, then handed the ring box to Harold. "Sounds like this one is the winner," he told him. "I can't wait to hear how the real proposal goes."

Amara looked down at her bare finger, then back up at Val, who seemed completely clueless to the fact that he'd just ripped an engagement ring off her hand and given it away. Not that he had any clue what she'd been thinking— hell, she didn't even know what she was thinking. She quickly cleared her throat and dropped her hand. "Yeah, good luck, Harold. I can't imagine she'd say no to a proposal like that one."

Harold nodded and tucked the ring box into his coat pocket. "Thanks again, Valentino. You're a good man giving me the old five-finger discount like that."

Val laughed and shook his head. "Five-finger discount is for shoplifters. I'm giving this to you, you're not stealing it."

"That's not the story I'm going to tell Ruthie," Harold said with a wink. "She likes bad boys, you know."

"Good lord, Harold," Val replied, shaking his head but laughing none the same. "You crack me up. Get out of here and go propose."

Harold tipped his cap to them before heading for the exit. "Thanks to you, too, young lady."

Amara gave him a wave and watched him leave. When she turned back to look at Val, he was rearranging some rings inside the display case in front of him. "Did you just give him that ring for free?"

Not that she didn't think he would, but the man had just lost half his inventory in a break-in. Now was hardly the time to be giving away more inventory.

He didn't look up at her, but rather kept going with his task at hand. "Yeah. Harold's a good guy. He bought all his jewelry for his first wife from my parents over the years. She died about five years back, and he met Ruthie last year. It's good to see him smiling again." He finished and finally looked up at her, before locking the display case. "What did you want to see me about?"

She blinked, trying to remember. "Uh..."

"Or did you just want to see me?" His signature devilish grin slid across his face and reminded her of how irritated she actually was with him.

Amara pulled his note out of her pocket. "You wish. What the hell was this?"

He took the card from her and read it. "Oh, they misspelled my name. It's R-o-s-s-i. No y."

She snatched it back from him and huffed. "I'm not talking about the spelling, Val. I'm talking about the comment of us spending the night together. Do you know what the delivery man probably thought when he read this?"

Val laughed. "That we spent the night together? Spoiler alert...we did. But, hey, while you're here, I just heard from Officer Powell, and the police want to meet with us on Saturday morning for an update on the case."

"They found something?" She lifted her brows, wondering why she hadn't gotten a call.

He shrugged. "They wouldn't say over the phone, just said it was routine. I'm guessing they're going to tell us they tried and are giving up. They just assume insurance will cover the damages, and we'll all move on."

"Will insurance cover everything?" she asked, the earlier heat of her indignation wearing off at the subject change. How the heck did he do that so easily? "Like all the lost inventory and all of the lost sales?"

"Doubtful," he replied. "But we'll figure it out. Did you get a security system yet?"

"I sent in a few requests for quotes this morning," she admitted. "I'll follow up tomorrow during business hours. I slept most of today. How are you not tired?"

"If that's an invitation to go to bed with you, Mara...well, I'll consider it." He gave her an exaggerated wink.

She groaned. "You are so beyond aggravating. I have plans tonight that I'm already late for."

With that, she turned on her heel and headed out of the

store. Glancing down at the time on her phone, she realized that she was definitely going to be late to meeting Nell at the diner, so she sent her a quick text to update her on her arrival time. Nell responded back with several knife emojis and a mind-blown emoji, which was her way of saying she was getting hangry.

She wasn't even sure why she'd stopped at the mall to confront Val when that hadn't even happened. Or had it? It was like everything in her brain turned to mush when he was around, and she hated the feeling. Except, she didn't really hate it at all, and *that* was what she really hated.

CHAPTER SIX

VALENTINO

"Well, that was a complete waste of time," Val announced to no one in particular as the police officers assigned to his case had finished filing out of the conference room they had been meeting in.

He'd come all the way down to the station on a Saturday morning—Valentine's Day, his busiest day, no less—for an update on the robbery only to hear exactly what he'd expected. They had nothing. No leads. No footage. No witnesses. No trace at local pawn shops of someone trying to fence the materials. In fact, they told him that their best guess was that whoever had stolen it had already pawned it off to a fence out of Detroit and it was in half a dozen cities by now.

They'd assured him that insurance would cover his loss and they'd be happy to write this all in their report to the company. Typical.

"I really thought they'd have something," Amara mused from where she was seated in one of the chairs at the conference room table. "Why couldn't they just tell you all that over the phone? Why did I need to be here?"

Val shrugged and stood up from his seat. He grabbed his coat and pulled it on. "Beats me, but I've got at least a dozen deliveries I need to get going on this afternoon."

"You do deliveries?" Amara frowned as she stood and followed suit, buttoning up her own jacket.

"For some higher end clients on special occasions, yeah," he replied. "You're welcome to come with me. I could always use an extra hand in free labor."

"Free labor?" She lifted her brows, as if daring him to stick by his statement.

He absolutely was. "Didn't you just hear the nice police officer? I'm down and out on my luck, Mara. Help a poor, robbed man out on the day of love, why don't you? Unless you have other plans for tonight?"

He wasn't sure why he'd even asked that because if she did have a date on Valentine's Day, he didn't want to know.

She laughed at his dramatic explanation and insinuation, but she didn't argue or say otherwise. "Jean's working the arcade today for me, so I guess I could help for a little. Not all day, though. And I need to go back and check in with her first."

That didn't answer at all if she had a date tonight, but he wasn't about to fish for an answer again and look desperate, even though they had bet on it when they'd played Space Invaders. He still didn't want to know.

"Perfect, because I have to grab everything at the store and prep the deliveries. See you there in, say, thirty minutes?" That would work just fine for him, and he'd be lying if he said he wasn't excited for the company. Not just any company, but hers specifically. He wasn't sure what had happened this week, but they'd become...friends.

Friends?

He didn't know what label to put on it, but he did know

that he liked being around her. He'd enjoyed their night together as mall rent-a-cops, and every interaction they'd had since. She felt like a partner-in-crime, or a teammate, or maybe that was just what friends were supposed to feel like? It wasn't that he didn't have any friends, but he certainly didn't make much time for them. He lived his life so independently that it didn't leave a lot of room for regular human connection outside of customers and one-night stands, or the occasional fling. He used to say that was because he didn't *need* anyone. He could handle life just fine on his own. But the last few days were beginning to make him wonder...maybe need was different than want. Maybe he wanted someone.

Maybe he wanted Mara Hart.

But about an hour and fifteen minutes later, he was rethinking that mental statement as they pulled up to the first house he was making a delivery to.

"This is where they live?" Amara was pointing at the gated entrance that prevented strangers from pulling into the large home's driveway of his first delivery.

It was set off from the street quite a bit, but he could see the peaks of the roof towering ahead of them. He hit the buzzer by the gate and waited to be let in.

"This place is massive."

"Yup, and we've got three deliveries at this stop, so he's a good customer." Val handed her a clipboard that had a list of deliveries on it. The speaker emitted a low baritone voice that asked for his name and reason for entrance. Once he provided that, he was buzzed in, and the gate opened in front of them. Val pulled up the long, windy driveway to the front door where a man in a carefully tailored black coat came out to meet him at the bottom of the front steps. "Mara, hand me the three boxes on top. Here's the key."

She checked the list, then looked in the back seat of his car at the locked trunk that was full of deliveries. Taking the key from him, she opened the trunk and pulled out the top three small red boxes delicately wrapped in white ribbon. "These are really cute. I love the wrapping job. Gifts for Marilyn, Cassie, and...Reggie?"

"Jewelers don't ask questions, Mara." He took the boxes from her. "I do know his wife's name is Marilyn, and they have a daughter—probably Cassie."

Amara's eyes were wide like she'd just found out an exciting piece of gossip and wanted to get to the bottom of it. "So, who is Reggie? What is in the box? Cufflinks? A toe ring? Oh my God, is it his secret lover? Is he closeted and the wife doesn't know it? Rich people are wild."

Val laughed and shook his head. "You watch too much Netflix. It's a dog collar. For their dog."

"For their 'dog,' mm-hmm. Sure." Amara put the words in fake air quotes with her fingers, clearly not buying it. "That's a convenient story."

He tried to muster a straight face as he got out of the car with the packages all lined up in a nice red bag with Kisses and Karats written on the front.

"Package for Mr. Davenport?" the gentleman in the suit at the bottom of the steps asked, extending his hand toward Val.

Val nodded, giving him the bag and instructing him to sign for the delivery before returning to the car and programming the next address into his GPS system.

"Where are we off to now?" Amara scanned her finger down his delivery list then stopped on a name. "Wait... Buxley. As in Senator Buxley? Like of our state?"

He grinned, casting her a wary side eye. "Are you going to be able to handle yourself?"

"I just don't understand why people need to jump through all these hoops one day a year to prove that they love each other. Real love doesn't need a trophy or some sort of physical evidence. Why can't people just be loving and kind to each other all year round?" She let out a sigh. "It's just all so commercialized now."

Val had heard her soapbox spiel more than once from plenty of people, but the old romantic soul in him never bought it. Everyone wanted to be acknowledged, and that's what he was in the business of—validating people and relationships. "You're quite the pessimist when it comes to love, aren't you?"

She shrugged, but he didn't look sideways to see what expression was on her face. "It's more of being a realist."

"I like to think of Valentine's Day as a moment of reflection on how much a person means to you—or who means what to you. We all go about our lives every day being so busy, trying to get that next promotion, meet our goals, whatever...it doesn't leave a lot of time for just sitting in the here and now. Just saying, hey, I love this person, I love having them in my life, and I want to celebrate that here and now, all on its own." Val turned down a side street toward their next destination. "Plus, not everyone has the verbal skills to communicate their feelings. Sometimes a gift is the most intimate way someone can express themselves, and that's still valid. That has worth and merit, just like words and actions."

She was quiet for a moment, seeming to be staring out the window. When they pulled up to the Senator's mansion, she handed him the large box full of multiple gifts and he ran it up just like he had at the last stop. They continued on like that for several more stops until his trunk was finally depleted.

"I think that's the last one," he said, closing and locking the lid. "Should I drop you at your place, or back at the store?"

"At the store, if you don't mind," she replied. "I left my car in the parking lot there. Don't want to be stranded this late at night, you know."

"Sure, but I'll drive home behind you and make sure you get there fine," he agreed.

She scrunched up her nose and chuckled. "Now you're trying to find out where I live?"

"Okay then, compromise. Put your number in my phone and call yourself. Text me when you're home safe. Otherwise, I'm following you." He handed her his cell phone as he pulled back into the parking lot at Yule Heights Shopping Mall.

Surprisingly, she didn't give him any pushback on that and took his phone without comment. A minute later, she handed it back to him. "I put it under Mara Hart. Not Amara."

"Perfect," he replied, parking in his usual reserved spot. "Come on. I have something for you back at the store, then I swear I'll stop bothering you."

Amara laughed as she climbed out of the car and joined him in the short walk up to the building. "You don't have to pay me. Free labor, remember?"

"Consider it a thank you gift instead then," he replied. When they arrived at Kisses and Karats, he went into the back room and pulled out a small silver and blue tennis bracelet from his safe. Returning to the main showroom, he slipped it into a small red decorative box and then presented it to Amara. "This is for you. Happy Valentine's Day."

She took it from his hands slowly, seemingly at a loss for

words, which was something he didn't see often with her. She opened the box and peered inside, gently fingering the silver chain between two fingers and gazing at the small blue rock attached to it. "Oh...wow. Thank you. It's very beautiful."

"It's a Larimar gemstone—or mineral pectolite, actually," he explained, excited to share about one of his favorite stones. Okay, so sometimes he got a little nerdy about rocks and gems. "Not costly or anything like that, but rich in meaning. Some people call it the dolphin stone, or the Atlantis stone, because supposedly one could only find it where Atlantis once was. It represents empathy and under-standing, and so I wanted you to have it." He took it out of the box and fastened it around her wrist. "Seeing everything you do around here for those kids—hell, even helping me out recently—it's pretty clear you have a big heart for other people, Mara. You're definitely a dolphin stone."

She was quiet again, just staring at the bracelet on her wrist. She placed her opposite hand over it and held it against her chest. "Thank you, Val."

"Good night, Mara." He wanted to pull her against him right then and there and kiss her until the morning. The way she looked so vulnerable and gentle right then felt like a gift, a special side of her that she was only letting him see. He wanted to tell her thank you, and that he hoped he'd see it again. Instead, he smiled and let out a low exhale. "Text me when you get home safe, okay?"

She nodded, thanked him again, and then headed out of the store.

"Happy Valentine's Day, Mara," he whispered to her retreating figure, even though she couldn't hear him.

Oh, how he wished she could really *hear* him.

CHAPTER SEVEN

AMARA

Tears stung at the edges of her eyes as Amara walked quickly back to the arcade and made a beeline for the back room. It was still open and full of customers, so she wasn't about to have an emotional breakdown on the arcade floor. Jean waved at her from a distance where she was helping a customer on the Skee-Ball machines, but Amara ignored her and pressed on.

When she got to the safety of the private back office in back, she closed the door behind her and let out a long, fast exhale that was promptly followed by a stream of small tears down both cheeks. *What the heck was wrong with her right now?* She looked down at the bracelet on her wrist, this beautiful new gift Val had just given her. Never in her life had she given two flying beeps about getting a gift from a guy, let alone jewelry. On Valentine's Day. It was beyond cliché. Gross, even.

But when he'd explained why he'd picked it, and what it meant to him...what he saw in her. Maybe there actually *was* something to gifts as an expression of love.

The word stuck in her throat—did she say (or think,

technically) love? Absolutely not. That's not at all where they were, or even remotely on the table. And yet, the word stayed lodged in her head and maybe a little further south in her heart.

Amara stood up straight and shook out her shoulders. She was being ridiculous. None of this was like her. None. She wasn't someone who went gooey-eyed over a handsome neighbor or tongue-tied over a beautiful trinket. But her mind went back to what she'd seen earlier with Harold, or how Val had helped her with the raccoon and finding estimates for security systems, or just the way that she felt lighter and happier when she was around him. She didn't feel nervous or like she had to put on a front, which was normally how she felt when she was dating someone.

But they weren't dating.

Why weren't they dating? He'd given her the sweetest gift she'd ever gotten in her life. She pulled her phone out of her pocket and glanced at her notifications—one missed call. It was his phone number that she'd called herself from. She clicked on it and saved it under his name, already planning what she'd text him when she got home.

Made it safely, thanks for the fun day! No, that was too lame.

I love the bracelet. You're incredible. Way too desperate.

Happy Valentine's Day, Valentino! I'm home. Oh, God, she should just not text him at all at this point.

I'm home. Want to come join me? Zero chance she'd have the courage to send that.

Amara sighed and pushed her phone back in her pocket before grabbing her keys and heading back out onto the arcade floor. She had at least a ten-minute drive to practice something better, but in reality, she was probably just going to text *home* and be done with it. Maybe throw in an emoji for some flare.

"Hey, Ms. Mara!" Marco waved to her from where he was standing in front of a race car game that his friend was playing. "Happy Valentine's Day!"

"Thanks, Marco," she replied, walking over to him since it was only a few steps out of the way. "You kids having fun tonight?"

"Eh, you know. Just trying to meet the ladies, pick up chicks, stuff like that." Marco shrugged his shoulders and ran his thumb across the bottom of his nose with a sly smirk on his lips.

Amara laughed and shook her head. "Christ, Marco. You're too young to even be thinking about stuff like that."

He grinned and his hands went to adjust the chain around his neck. Amara glanced down and noticed the clasp on the end, and suddenly her whole body felt like it had gone stiff.

"Hey, uh, Marco..." Amara wasn't sure how to even get started, but she recognized the clasp on Marco's chain as clear as day. It was the same clasp on the bracelet she was wearing now—the Kisses and Karats signature clasp on all of Val's necklaces, chains, and bracelets. It was a tiny silver triangle with the letter K etched in the middle, and she'd only ever seen it in one place. "That's a really nice chain you have there. Is it new?"

He looked away from her suddenly, clearing his throat. "Yeah, uh. It's a gift. My older brother gave it to me for my birthday."

She put a hand on his upper arm and gently guided him a few steps away from his friends so that she could lower her voice and speak privately. "Marco...where did your brother get that chain?"

Marco ran a hand across the back of his neck, still unable to make direct eye contact with her. "I can't say, okay? Ms. Mara, can you please just drop it? It's just a dumb gold chain."

She frowned at his response, but just dropping things had never been her way of operating. She needed to get him away from his friends so that she could get the truth out of him. "Hey, you know, you almost hit twenty-thousand points. Want to come check out the Nintendo Switches?"

His eyes lit up and he grinned, finally looking at her. "Hell, yeah. Hey, guys, I'm going to go get my Switch."

He followed her up to the front easily and as soon as he was far enough away from his friends, she stopped them both in their path. "Marco, I know that chain came from Kisses and Karats next door. You didn't have it earlier this week before the store was robbed. Do you know something about that robbery?"

Marco swallowed hard, his eyes darting around the arcade probably trying to assess who was nearby or in listening distance. "Ms. Mara..."

She cut him off. "I need you to tell me. If you did this, Marco, we can talk to the courts and get help. We can ask for leniency, something. But you need to return everything you took."

"I didn't take anything, I swear," he replied adamantly. "It was...look, my brother said I needed to just flip the circuit breaker so the power would go off. That's all he asked me to do. I didn't know he was going to rob the jewelry store with his friends. He's my brother, you know? I couldn't say no."

Shit. Amara was never going to hear the end of it from Val when he heard that her store's circuit breaker had been the culprit's entire in to rob his store. "They came through my store?"

"I guess," Marco replied, his hands wringing the hem of his shirt in a nervous gesture. "I'm sorry, Ms. Mara. I didn't mean for any of that to happen. Are you going to tell the police?"

She shook her head. "You're a good kid, Marco, but I think you need to be the one to go tell the owner at the jewelry store what happened."

His eyes went wide. "What? No. I can't. He'll have me arrested!"

"Listen, I'll go with you. Val is a reasonable guy. I'm sure we can figure out some way of solving this." Amara put her hand on the back of his shoulder. "Can I go with you over there now?"

He looked like he was about ready to throw up, but he finally nodded and followed her out of the arcade to the store next door. When they got to the showroom, he paused and looked ready to bolt.

Amara gave him a gentle pat on the shoulder. "You can do this, Marco."

"Maybe he's not here," Marco attempted to stall. "It says it's closed."

She knocked on the store gate anyway, knowing Val wouldn't have had time to leave that quickly. A few seconds later, the gate lifted with a loud racket and Val was standing in front of both of them.

"Hey, I thought you were going home," he said, smiling at Amara. "Who's this?"

"Val, meet Marco. Marco, this is Val." Amara squared her shoulders and gave Val a pleading look, hoping he'd get the message without her having to tell him to go easy on the kid. "Marco might know some information about the robbery."

Val's eyes widened and he crossed his arms over his

chest as he took in the young boy for a second time. This time his gaze lingered on the chain around Marco's neck, and she had no doubt that he recognized it every bit as much as she had. "Well, what is it?"

In a complete explosion of verbal diarrhea, Marco explained how his brother had told him to trip the circuit breaker at the arcade, which had turned out all the power. When Marco had gotten home from the arcade later that night, he'd discovered his brother and his friends in their living room with all the stolen jewelry and merchandise and once he'd seen the news, he put two and two together. His brother had even given him the chain as a thank you gift of sorts for his part in it, but Marco swore repeatedly he hadn't known that that was what was going to happen.

"You've got to believe me, sir. I would never do something like that," Marco said for the tenth time. "I'm so sorry. Here, here. Take the chain back."

He lifted it from around his neck and handed it to Val.

Val took it and placed it on top of a nearby display case. He kept his back to them for a minute or two, and even Amara was beginning to feel nervous about what his next steps might be. She didn't want to see anything happen to Marco, and she certainly didn't want to see him arrested... but what the hell was the protocol in a situation like this?

"Listen, Marco," Val began as he turned around and faced them again. "You seem like a good kid with prospects. Your brother could be, too, but he's going down a bad path. I am going to have to report this information so that police can apprehend him."

"But then he's going to know I told you." Marco's voice turned into a high-pitched whine. "Please, sir. He's my only family. He's all I've got."

Val looked conflicted, his gaze finding hers with a silent plea as if begging her to tell him what to do.

"I think he's right, Marco. We do need to tell the police what your brother did, but it doesn't have to come from you," she pitched in, trying to think on her feet. "Maybe there's another way—like maybe he told someone else. Or maybe he posted something online? Or...I don't know."

"Instagram!" Marco's eyes lit up and he pulled his phone out of his pocket. He began clicking through apps and scrolling until he found what he was looking for, then turned the screen toward Val. "He posted a story wearing the stuff from the robbery."

Val took the phone and examined it. "Yeah, that definitely looks like my merchandise. Why would he post this online?"

"He said it looked cool." Marco shrugged. "I mean, it is kind of bad ass."

"Jewelry store owner here," Val reminded the young boy. "That's my property he's wearing."

"Right, right." Marco nodded. "Well, I'll send you a screenshot of it, okay? The police can say that's how they found it. Nobody needs to know I said anything. Right?"

The young boy looked so hopeful, and Amara had no idea if they were doing the right thing or not. But she'd known Marco for over a year now, and she wanted to believe he was better than this. She *knew* he was. This kid had a good heart, and he was smart as a whip. He could have a lot of different futures that didn't look like the path his brother was currently walking.

"Send them to me now via Airdrop," Val told Marco, holding his phone up toward him. "I'll take care of the rest. You go back over to the arcade and play, okay?"

Marco did what he said quickly and then scurried out of the jewelry store as fast as he could.

"Thanks for not going hard on him," she said to Val once Marco was out of sight. "He's a good kid, but his situation is difficult. His brother is his guardian. If his brother gets arrested, I'm not sure what that will mean for Marco or his living arrangements."

Val rubbed a hand across the back of his neck and let out a sigh. "I hate this world sometimes. Nothing is ever black and white. I don't have a choice though, Mara. I have to turn this evidence over to the police. It would basically be insurance fraud and a crime if I withheld it knowingly."

"I know, I know," she agreed. "This is just...it's so shitty."

"Thanks for bringing him over here and getting him to tell me all that. That couldn't have been easy." Val looked down at his phone, scrolling through the pictures of screenshots that Marco had sent him. "I'm going to forward these to Officer Powell now. Get home safe, okay?"

"Thanks." She paused a moment longer, then inhaled slowly. "Happy Valentine's Day to you, too, by the way."

Val grinned, offering her a wink before she turned and walked away so that he wouldn't have a chance to say anything further. She didn't know what the hell she wanted him to say, but she darn well knew what she wanted him to do. She wanted him to wrap his arms around her right then and there, pull her against his rock-hard chest and abs, and kiss her until she experienced again every bit of emotion that she'd felt when he'd slipped that bracelet on her wrist.

But instead, she was going to get in her car and run through eighteen different scenarios about what she should text him when she did finally make it home safe.

CHAPTER EIGHT

VALENTINO

"That's it?" Val frowned as the police officer laid out the pieces of jewelry in front of him at the precinct that they'd recovered from Marco's house.

Sure enough, his older brother had done the deed, and the moment the police came in, he'd confessed and surrendered. It was a real shame, honestly, because the entire thing could have been avoided. As frustrated as he was for how he was faring in this situation, he felt guilty as hell for taking Marco's only guardian.

"The rest was either pawned, stolen, or given away. Apparently he threw a few parties where he was showing it off and passing some of it out. Honestly, it's going to be impossible to trace it all." The officer pointed to the jewelry that they had recovered. "This is actually a pretty good return."

"Yeah," Val agreed. He hadn't expected to ever see any of his pieces again, so the fact that he had some right here in front of him was still a win. "What's going to happen to the kid?"

"His pre-trial hearing is this week, so we'll see what the

judge says. I'm sure they'll take into consideration anything you request, but we are talking grand larceny." The officer handed him a clipboard. "Here, sign that I'm releasing this inventory to you."

Val signed the document and began packing his pieces away in the jewelry bags and boxes he'd brought with him at the police officer's directive. "What about his little brother, Marco? What will happen to him?"

The police officer shook his head. "I don't have any information on that, but if he had a ward, then probably the state will get involved. Foster care system."

"Can you maybe get my information to his case worker? Just in case? I want to follow up and make sure he's fine." Val handed a business card to the police officer. "I know that probably sounds strange, but I just want to make sure he's okay."

"Sure, I can pass it to the caseworker. I can't make him call you, though." The officer took the card and stuck it to the report. "Everything will work out eventually. It always does."

Val wasn't entirely sure about that these days, but he didn't argue the point. He'd spent the last six days working with police to get everything resolved after he'd discovered the news from Marco. In that time, he had to have his store closed and an insurance rep came out to go over all their findings. The insurance company wanted to make sure to remove the value of any returned pieces from the check he was going to get—which still didn't make up for the full loss, but it was moot at this point.

The frustrating part about all of it, however, had been that he hadn't been able to see Amara all week. She'd texted on Valentine's Day when she'd gotten home safe as she'd promised—simply just the one word, home. But since then, he'd barely gotten more than one or two words out of her when he'd check in. He kept her up to date on the case, and she was encouraging, but there was something lost in the virtual exchange compared to when they were standing in front of one another.

Now that everything was summed up in a neat little package, however, he wanted to go see her. He returned with the items to his store and made sure everything was securely locked away before he made his way over to the arcade. It was busy, as it always was on weekends, and he could see Amara's employee at the main counter helping guests. He scanned the room full of games for her, but didn't see her brightly colored, pink-and-red-hued hair anywhere.

Getting an idea, he pulled out his phone and opened his Tinder app. With a few quick changes to his profile's bio, he began swiping within a one-mile radius to see if he could find her. Sure enough, three swipes later and her picture popped up.

Amara, 32. Just a dolphin lost at sea.

He paused as he read her tag line, because it hadn't said that before. Last time he'd seen her profile it had said something about chicken nuggets—odd, but it had made him laugh and definitely remember it. Was this because of the bracelet he'd given her? His heart started to beat harder against his chest, and he wondered if this meant what he hoped it meant.

He swiped on her picture and a notification appeared stating that they had matched on the app. He clicked the message button and began typing out a message to her.

I came here on porpoise hoping to find you.

He hit send, and then waited. A little series of dots popped up on the screen indicating that she was typing, and her response was visible seconds later.

That was mammally funny.

He grinned at her use of a pun back to his pun joke. He decided to let her know that he was here and looking for her. *In the mood for a game of Ms. Pac Man?*

See you there. Bet you'll recognize the high scorer.

Val laughed, because there was rarely a conversation with her where she didn't toss in her random trivia about her previous championship title on Ms. Pac-Man. But he indulged her anyway and wound his way around the other games until he got to the machine he was looking for.

He pressed the button in the front, and the high scores appeared on the screen. Of course, the top one just said MARA H., but the ones after that were what caught his attention.

The second high scorer was named B. MINE. The third was VAL ENTINE. The fourth was V. ROSSI. Which was definitely his name and initial. He frowned, trying to decipher if it was a message, or if someone actually just had really strange initials and a name very similar to his.

"Do you like it?" a voice came from behind him.

He turned to see Amara standing there with a sly grin on her face. Her hair had a new streak in it—this time it was a lime green. He wanted to run his hand through her hair, hell, he wanted to run his hands over every part of her. But he didn't move. "What does it say?"

He wanted to hear her say it. He needed to hear her say it.

She stepped closer to the machine and pointed at the high scores. "It says, Be mine, Valentine."

"Mara, are you trying to say something?" He leaned in closer to her, closing the distance between them and letting his hand rest on her hip, guiding her closer. His voice lowered to just above a whisper. "Are you asking me to be your Valentine?"

She tilted her chin up until her lips were parallel with his. "Valentine's Day is over," she teased, and he could feel her breath against his face. Sweet, like cinnamon. "But I'm still available next year if you'll have me."

Val wrapped his arm around her back and pulled her body to his. His voice dropped lower, a gravelly quality to it now. "I don't think I can wait fifty-one more weeks to kiss you, Mara."

"Please don't," she breathed back in response.

And so, he didn't.

Cheers came from around them as kids and teens clapped, but he didn't even notice because all he could understand in that moment was how incredible it felt to have his arms around the woman he'd found himself falling head over heels for. He lifted her up off her feet and spun her in a circle, never once breaking their kiss, before he finally set her back down on the ground.

"It's a date," he finally said to her question. "I'll be your Valentine."

"You kind of already were," she joked, squeezing his hand. "We just hadn't made it official."

"Are we official now?" he asked, dipping down to kiss her once more.

She lingered on his kiss for a moment, breathing a soft smile when she broke away. "Like Harold and Ruth official."

"You can't just throw the corsage at her and run away, Marco." Amara straightened the young boy's tie as he stood in front of her. "You have to hand it to her nicely and ask her to dance, get her some punch, and make sure she gets home safe at the end of the night."

"That's so boring though," Marco whined. He looked over at the couch where Val was seated with his feet up on the coffee table, drinking a glass of red wine. "Val, will you tell her that people don't do that old school dance thing anymore? It's all about prom-posals and fancy asks and who's got the best outfit and stuff like that. You know, you're a jeweler!"

"He's got a point there, babe. Kids are really into those flash dance mobs and trendy viral video proposals and stuff. I don't think they sit on the sidelines as much as we used to at school dances." Val took another sip of wine. "But I wouldn't be much help there. I have no idea how Mara is even still with me."

She laughed and turned to give him the stink eye, then lifted her hand and waggled her fingers at him. The black opal stone on her ring finger shimmered under the lights in their family room. "You're stuck with me for good now," she reminded him.

They'd moved in together about nine months ago when Val had agreed to become a temporary foster parent for Marco while his older brother served out his jail sentence for the robbery. They'd only been dating a few months at that point, but there was zero doubt in her mind that she not only wanted to be with Val for the rest of her life, but also be part of the weird little family they'd created.

And she couldn't wait until later tonight when they were alone, and she could tell him about the new addition they'd created for their little family, who would be joining them in about seven and a half months. They hadn't talked about the timing around kids when they'd gotten married at the courthouse on their sixth month anniversary, but this all felt right. It was fast. It was insane. It was completely out of character for anything she'd ever done before, but there was no doubt...this was right. This was her family.

Amara ran a hand over her stomach, feeling a flutter of excitement race through her.

"Okay, the tie is as straight as it's going to get." She stepped back and looked at Marco with a proud smile. Tonight was the Valentine's Day Dance at school and he'd never gone to a dance with a date before. Somehow, he'd summoned the courage this year to ask his science class partner, Elena, to go with him and she'd said yes. "Remember—ten o'clock curfew. No alcohol or anything worse. If you need anything, call me with the code word *melon* and I'll pick you up immediately. No questions asked."

"I know, I know." Marco groaned and rolled his eyes as

any typical fourteen-year-old might. "I'll see you guys later. Have fun on your date night, too!"

She waved him off as his friend's mom pulled up out front with a van full of teenagers carpooling to the dance. Amara waved to her and shouted thank you, then she returned inside to find Val in the kitchen. He was pulling a tray of salmon out of the oven that he'd made and stuffed with blue cheese, spinach, and a white wine burr blanc sauce. The smell was already making her stomach growl, which wasn't unusual since she was hungrier than normal these days.

"It's almost ready. I set the table." Val placed the fish back in the oven for a few more minutes. "Would you like another glass of wine?"

He looked over to where her glass was sitting on the tabletop untouched. "Oh, you didn't finish it yet. Guess I'm outpacing you," he joked, holding up his own glass, which was close to empty.

She didn't say anything, but his gaze caught hers and he paused, the glass at his lips.

He lowered it, staring at her. "Wait a minute..."

A smile spread across her face, and she looked down at her stomach, her hands cupping the small bump that was probably mostly bloating at this early stage. "I don't think I'll be having any wine for a little bit," she admitted. "Maybe for Christmas?"

"You're pregnant?" The words left his lips in a whisper, a smile so wide that it lit up his eyes. "We're pregnant?"

She nodded, because if she dared try to speak in that moment, she was pretty sure she'd start crying.

He placed his wine glass down on the counter and lifted her up into his arms and spun her around in a circle. "Mara, this is the best Valentine's Day gift I've ever received."

"I love you, Val," she whispered against his lips. "I can't wait to have a family with you."

"You're already my family," he replied. "I love you, Mara Rossi."

She kissed him again. "Happy Valentine's Day."

EXCERPT FROM NUDES

A HOLLYWOOD ROMANCE

PROLOGUE

Aria woke with a jolt, looking around the dark bedroom. As her senses slowly began to adjust, she looked for the source of whatever had disturbed her. Her cell phone vibrated against the surface of her nightstand, the screen lit so brightly it cast a square light onto the ceiling above.

Yawning, Aria grabbed for it. She glanced over at the man in bed next to her, her heart filling with warmth at the sight of his sleeping form.

Finally focusing on her phone, she realized she had dozens of missed texts, calls, and emails.

"What the hell?" she whispered to herself, sitting up.

Aria, are you awake? WAKE UP NOW.

Don't look at the news. We need to talk. 911.

Is that you on E! News? Did you allow that?

OMG, ARIA! WHAT THE HELL?

What did you do?!?! This is career suicide!

Her heart began to race, panic swarming her every cell as she quickly clicked out on a website link her best friend sent her. A photo popped up, and then another, and another, and another, and Aria knew exactly what she was looking at.

Herself.

Nude.

Aria could barely breathe, trembling as she searched social media and entertainment news sites. The photos were everywhere. She was everywhere. Her breasts, her body, her love life on full display for the world to see.

It would have been bad enough if they'd just been images of her posing, but these were pornographic. These were her in her most intimate moments with a man she'd...

A sob stuck in her throat. *Did he do this?*

She looked at the man still sleeping beside her, fear gripping her heart.

This couldn't be happening.

CHAPTER ONE

"Wait until you meet our lead." The heavyset producer's eyes glinted with excitement as he spoke. He brought a sandwich up to his lips, taking a bite and continuing around a mouthful of food. "She's only had small roles up until this film, but she's up-and-coming. No doubt about it. Aria Rose is poised to take the world by storm come Oscar season."

Ben didn't reply, too distracted watching the producer trying to wipe a blob of mayonnaise off his tie. Arthur Atwood was a large man with a messy comb-over and an ill-fitting suit, which must have been a deliberate choice since Ben knew Arthur made a handsome salary.

Is he licking his tie?

His new right-hand man was actually licking mayonnaise off his tie. Not a good sign. Ben made a mental note never to ask Arthur to have a meeting over lunch at his desk again.

"Bugger, it's in there good," Arthur muttered in his thick English accent, dropping his tie and slapping his hands on his knees. "All right. Enough of that. Ready for a tour of the studio?"

"Very," Ben replied, balling up the parchment paper his own sandwich had been wrapped in and tossing it into the wastebasket beneath his desk. He stood, rolling his shoulders and stretching his neck from side to side.

They'd spent the morning touring the corporate offices on the lot of Shepherd Film Studios where Ben would be officially starting in two weeks as the company's new chief executive officer. He had agreed to come in on Friday to tour everything and meet the crew on their final day of filming—but the pressure was already on.

One of the oldest movie production companies in Hollywood, Shepherd Film Studios was well respected, but struggled to adapt to new changes in the industry—the rise of streaming services, quicker distribution on the internet, and other changes that appealed to younger generations.

Maguire Industries had recently purchased the studio and placed Ben in charge to fix that. He had one year to prove to the board at Maguire that he could turn Shepherd Films back into a thriving production company or they'd dismantle the company and sell it off for profit.

He was Shepherd Films last resort, and thank goodness, too. No one else in Hollywood was desperate enough to throw him a lifeline. Being an embarrassing public spectacle for the last two years had been by far one of the biggest setbacks in his professional life to date—and his personal life was to blame.

Fucking divorce.

"Have you seen any of her movies?" Arthur held the door to the office open for him, and together they headed down the hallways of the main offices. "She's a bombshell—literally one of the most gorgeous women I've ever seen."

"Aria Rose?" Ben replied, racking his brain for a mental image of the actress. "I've seen a few. Very pretty. She's very talented but never been a lead."

"*Scarlet's Letters* is her first starring role, and she's perfect for it. We can watch the dailies from today's filming, and you'll see what I mean. We were really lucky to score her for this film."

Ben had wondered about that, too. Aria wasn't necessarily A-list, but she was an up-and-coming fan favorite among millennial and younger generations. Her social media attention was nonstop, and there was an almost cult following to her that had made Hollywood execs begin to take notice. Yet, he'd seen the budget this morning. She was being vastly underpaid for this film, and he wasn't sure why.

They passed the guards at the front desk of the main offices and stepped out into the sun. "How did your team manage to sign her?" Ben asked.

"Sheer luck, I'd gather. She was following the script around—or so I heard. Determined to be part of it, though I can't say why exactly. The script is great—historical World War II romance with a Hester Prynne theme—and we're already getting some Oscar buzz from it. Still, it's a long shot, and it's nothing like her previous films."

Ben pulled a pair of sunglasses from his suit pocket and placed them over his eyes. The bright Los Angeles sun was beating down on them as they climbed onto a golf cart to traverse the large lot to the studios. "Sounds like we're the lucky ones, then."

"You've got that right," Arthur agreed, taking the driver's seat since Ben was still mostly unfamiliar with the area.

A few minutes later, their golf cart pulled up outside a large warehouse-type building that read *STUDIO E* in large black letters across the top. Ben climbed out and followed

Arthur to a small door off to the side, a red light lit above the door.

Arthur pointed to the light. "That means they're filming, so not a peep." He placed a finger to his mouth, indicating they needed to be quiet.

Ben nodded, and they entered the building only to be immediately shrouded in darkness. It might be his first day at Shepherd Films, but Ben was no stranger to movie sets and felt immediately at ease as they carefully made their way over to where the camera crew was.

Ben's father, Roger Lawson, was a highly sought after cameraman who'd taken a career most people overlooked and became the best. He'd taught Ben to do the same—excel in everything by putting his whole heart into every project, no matter how small or large. As a young boy, he'd spent many a summer day with his father at work, learning the business of not only filming, but creating movies, in general.

Newly thirty years old, Ben had spent the last decade putting his father's words into practice, rising through the ranks to become one of the hottest names in film produc-tion. He only wished his father was still alive to see his ascent, or at least, he had wished that until his ex-wife smeared his name through the tabloids during their divorce.

Never fall in love with an actress. The one rule his father had told him before he died that Ben had ignored. Lesson learned.

"Am I to be punished for helping a fellow human being?" A strong female voice broke through the silence around them.

Ben stepped around a crowd of onlookers to see the set. Behind him was an entire crew, and not a single dry eye. The emotion on everyone's face surprised him. Following their attention to the main set, he saw the set was a bedroom. Sitting on the edge of the bed was a tall, broad-shouldered man with his head in his hands, wearing a soldier's uniform from the 1940's.

In front of the downtrodden soldier was a statuesque blonde, her hair flowing down her back in one long, chunky braid. Pieces of her golden mane escaped the braid, framing her face and highlighting her soft, pink cheeks. Pale blue-gray eyes brimmed with tears as she folded her hands over her heart.

"I won't lie, James," she continued, her voice softer now. "I can't."

The soldier suddenly stood, gripping the woman by her upper arms. "You have to lie, Anna. Your life is at stake—my life, *our life*. You'll be imprisoned, and everything we've dreamt of will be over."

She steeled herself, her jaw tightening. "If this is real...if our love is real...then we'll survive this. Without the lies, the tricks, the falsehoods. We can survive this, James."

Ben felt a swelling in his chest, a lump in his throat. He wasn't even sure what the storyline was about, and yet, he was captivated by the woman in front of the cameras. Her presence was powerful...*she* was powerful.

"No, Anna." He dropped her arms and stepped back, a look of disgust on his face. "We can't survive this. Not if you choose their lives over mine...over ours."

The blonde shook her head slowly, her hand now on her stomach as if she might be sick. "You can't mean that, James. You can't make me pick between loving you and my purpose in life."

"It's them...or it's me. Now or never, Anna."

Ben focused on the actress's face, expecting to see her acquiesce to the steely-delivered ultimatum. Instead, her chin pushed up and she inhaled deeply. Everything about her posture and stance screamed strength, and yet, in the exact same moment, those blue-gray eyes ached with pain. Ben nearly forgot he was watching actors because her portrayal was so genuine...she was so genuine.

"Goodbye, James." Her voice was gentle, but resolute.

The soldier's nostrils flared angrily, before he slowly shook his head. "Goodbye, Anna." With that, he walked out of the door and left her standing alone in the bedroom.

She waited a moment, staring after him. Her hand slowly lifted to her lips, covering her mouth as a loud sob ripped from her throat. In an excruciating display, her body dipped forward slightly before completely crumpling in on itself. She fell against the edge of the bed, sobbing into its sheets, as the lights on set dimmed.

"Cut!" the director yelled. "Holy fuck. That was amazing, Aria!"

The blond actress pushed up off the bed, smiling and wiping the tears from her cheeks. Everyone in the studio erupted into applause, and Ben joined in. She deserved every second of it after that performance.

A surge of excitement ran through Ben's body—he could do this. With acting like this, there was no way their movie wouldn't be a success. There was no way he wouldn't be able to bring this studio success within the year with a film like this.

"Hey, Russell," Arthur called out to the director and ushered Ben over to him. "Meet our new studio head, Ben Lawson."

Ben extended a hand to the grungy looking man with long, curly black hair to his shoulders. "Good to meet you, Russell."

"Please, call me Russ. I'm Russ Rains, director. I'm sure you've heard of me." He donned a cocky smile. Metal and bracelets around his wrists made a clanking sound as they shook hands—a not too unusual fashion choice in this city.

"I have," Ben admitted, though he didn't really like this man's ego already. It was certainly nothing unusual in Hollywood, and Ben had met the type many a time before. Russell Rains was a legitimately well-known director with several big box office hits under his belt, though it had been many years since his last. "Your work is amazing, Russ."

"Thank you, Benji," Russ said with an obnoxious chuckle. "Come on. Let me introduce you to our leads."

"I'll meet you back at the office," Arthur told Ben. "Have fun on set!"

Ben followed Russell onto the bedroom set where the actress he'd been so captivated by was hugging the soldier who'd just broken her heart.

"You were amazing, Travis," she said to him, pulling back from their embrace to smile at him.

Something inside Ben stirred—irritation, anger? He wasn't sure, but he didn't like seeing the man's arms around the beautiful blonde.

"Sweet pea, come meet our new studio head," Russ called out to Aria, who visibly bristled at his demand. Ben made a mental note to ask about the director's dynamic with the actors later. "This here is Benji."

"*Ben* Lawson," Ben corrected the director, extending his hand to the woman.

"Aria Rose," she replied, taking his hand with a gentle squeeze. Her fingers were small and warm around his, and there was something sad about letting go. "Pleased to meet you, Mr. Lawson. This is my co-star, Travis Peters."

The soldier shook his hand next. "Good to meet you, sir."

"Please, call me Ben," he instructed them both. "Travis,

you were fantastic. And, Aria, I have to admit that your performance just now was incredible. I was unbelievably moved."

Her pale pink cheeks darkened as she looked down at her hands. "Thank you."

"I have no doubt this movie will be phenomenal."

Russ slapped a hand on Ben's back. "Hell, yeah. That was our last scene, so we're officially wrapped." The director stepped away from them and yelled to the entire crew. "It's a wrap, fuckers!"

Ben didn't even cringe at the man's abrasiveness this time.

The crew clapped and cheered, and everyone was hugging and high-fiving each other. A swarm of people came onto the bedroom set to congratulate Aria, pushing Ben backward as he watched her gracefully accept their praise.

In fact, he couldn't take his eyes off her, and it only had a little to do with how unbelievably attracted he was to her. As he stepped to the side, he watched how she smiled, laughing and embracing her co-workers. It was captivating. Aria commanded a room, not just when she was acting, but as herself. Her eyes danced and shone as she spoke to the crew and other actors, her smile wide and transformative.

He felt drawn to who she was, not just what he saw, and it was intoxicating. Though, what he saw was certainly breathtaking. Gorgeous wasn't enough to describe this woman, or the way her long neck dipped into thin shoulders and a deep collarbone. Her breasts pushed against the dark red dress she was wearing that highlighted her hourglass silhouette, and her golden braid hung down over her shoulder with a weight and visible softness he'd never seen before.

Someone bumped Ben's shoulder as they rushed in her direction, bringing Ben back to reality. *What the fuck am I doing?* He was barely six months out of a long divorce and had sworn off women entirely for now. And an actress? That was not happening. No way would he repeat his previous mistake twice. Not to mention that he was her boss, essentially, and that it would be a major conflict of interest. That was even assuming she was single and interested in him, which...

Why am I even thinking about this? Ben shook the thought from his head, unsure when the last time was that he'd ever felt this foggy-headed over a woman.

Aria's laughter peeled through the air just then, melodic and joyous. Ben swallowed hard, shoving his hands in his pockets and heading for the door. He had to get out of there. Now.

He wouldn't let himself fall for another actress, not even one as beautiful as Aria Rose.

"CONGRATULATIONS, SWEETIE!" Betty Reynolds, Aria's mother, rushed over to her and threw her arms around her neck. "You were *amazing*. There was no doubt, of course, but my God, sweetheart! You're a star!"

"Ma! Too tight!" Aria gasped, but hugged her mother back.

Her mother held her at arm's length. "Look at you." She exhaled loudly, smiling dreamily at her. "Seriously, Aria. You are so talented."

Aria felt her cheeks heat and looked away, never one to be very comfortable with praise. "Ma..."

"I'm serious, baby girl. The most talented actress I've ever seen."

Aria laughed, but welcomed her mother's input anyway. At times, Betty Reynolds may be overly involved in her life, but she'd prefer that than to not have her at all. In fact, Betty was not only her mother but her manager. She'd hired her years ago and hadn't regretted it for a second, probably because no one would ever work as hard or fight as fiercely for her. Aria credited a lot of her own success to her mother for that. "Thank you, Ma. I'm happy we're wrapped, though."

"Well, given your history on set..." Betty glanced toward the director, Russell Rains, who was currently talking to one of the cameramen. "It's understandable that you'd want to be out of here."

Aria pulled her gaze from Russ, her stomach turning at the thought. No one else in her family but her mother knew that she'd dated Russell for the first three months of filming. He was brilliant and intense, and she'd gotten swept up in the passion of it all, mixing her real emotions into the scripted life he led. She'd been so naive—a harsh fact she'd learned when she'd found him with an intern's head bobbing up and down in his lap.

Since breaking things off with Russell, she'd found him unbelievably difficult to work with. He'd made it very clear he resented the fact that she'd initiated their end—as if she was the first woman to ever reject him. It had made for an uncomfortable last few months of filming, but she'd done her best to ignore his passive aggressive barbs and blatant advances.

All things considered, she was really happy with her own performance, even if she hadn't seen the final product yet.

"This movie is going to be big, Aria. I can *feel* it."

Aria wrapped an arm around her mother's shoulders as they walked in the direction of the dressing rooms. "From your lips to God's ears."

When they arrived at her room, a small room with no windows on the second floor of a long row of dressing rooms, Aria dropped down on the couch with a big sigh. "I could sleep forever."

"Why don't you take a nap before heading home?" Betty

asked, her eyes on her watch. "I've got to get home to relieve your father's nurse for the evening."

"Oh, go, go. Don't let me keep you." Aria pulled her feet onto the couch and pushed a pillow under her head, curling up for a nap. "I probably will rest my eyes for a minute."

Betty grabbed a throw blanket off a nearby chair and draped it over her. "Okay, sweetheart. I love you."

"Love you, Ma," Aria said, already drifting off to sleep. They'd been filming since four in the morning today, trying to finish the last scene. Now that it was over, she felt like she could sleep for days.

Darkness fell over the room, and Aria felt her body relax, slipping out of consciousness. Minutes, hours, she wasn't sure how long she'd slept before she was jolted awake.

"Oh, shit. Were you sleeping?"

Sitting up, Aria blinked and rubbed her eyes. Russell was standing in the doorway of her dressing room, a wicked grin on his face.

"What do you want, Russ?" She kept her tone flat, her teeth clenched.

"You coming to the wrap party tonight?"

Aria yawned, checking the clock on the wall. She'd apparently been sleeping for three hours—much longer than a nap. "Yeah, I'm going."

She was feeling refreshed after the extra hours of rest, and she did want to celebrate with the crew—even if that meant enduring another few hours of her ex-boyfriend.

Russ glanced up and down the hallway outside the room, then stepped in and closed the door behind him. "Hey, maybe we should have a celebration of our own..."

Aria immediately got to her feet. "Get. Out."

"Come on, baby," he cooed, crossing the room. "Don't

you miss us? The film's wrapped, and we can get back to being us outside of work."

"*Us* was over the moment I caught you fooling around with an intern," she seethed, instantly angry that he still couldn't take a hint.

Russ's face glowered, going from sexual to angry. "Whatever. I've got a good memory." He winked at her and gestured first to his head, and then to his crotch as if he was jerking off.

Aria's stomach turned. "You're disgusting."

He shrugged while he walked back to the door, nonchalantly. Looking back over his shoulder, his face split into a wicked smile. "You'll be back. D-List actresses always come back for this dick when they realize I'm the best they'll ever have."

"Fuck you," Aria shot out, crossing her arms over her chest.

With his signature sinister smile, he walked out of the dressing room.

Aria's insides boiled. *Slime.* He was complete and utter slime. Clearly, she'd lost her damn mind when she'd briefly dated him. She'd been so easily mesmerized by his talent as a director, and he'd taught her so much. She'd thought it was just innocent, but all those extra late night lessons had turned into him hitting on her and her...just going with it.

Groaning, Aria dropped back onto the couch. *God, I'm so stupid.* She couldn't believe she'd been fooled by someone as blatantly slimy as him.

"Hey, Aria!" A silver-haired beauty bounced into the room through the doorway Russ had just exited.

"Hi, Steele," Aria greeted her makeup artist and hair stylist, who was really more like her best friend after spending every day together over the past few months of filming. Steele was her full name—or so she insisted—*like Cher*, she always said.

Steele collapsed onto the couch next to her, leaving a puff of glitter in the air. "Today is the absolute worst."

"What? Why?" Aria turned to her friend, pulling her legs up on the couch to face her.

Steele was uniquely gorgeous, the kind of beauty that was all personality, too. Brightly dyed silver hair, colorful makeup, ears lined with half a dozen earrings each, and vibrantly colored clothes made her stand out in any room. Her always exuberant attitude matched her style, and the two had quickly grown close.

"It's our last day," Steele said, her voice exaggeratedly whining. "Friendship over!"

Aria laughed, tipping her head back at her friend's dramatics. "Our friendship is not over! It's the last day of filming, but you know I'm going to need you again. There's still the photo shoot for promos for the film. There's the red carpet look. Press events. There's a ton of things I still need you for."

"Oh, great," Steele teased, tossing her hands up. "So, we're only friends because you still need me."

"Aside from being the best makeup artist and hair stylist in town, I have no use for you," Aria said in mock seriousness. "Honestly, you're just in the way otherwise."

Steele squawked. "Bitch."

"You know I'm kidding!" Aria leaned her head on Steele's shoulder, hugging her arm. "I love you, girl. We're still friends even if we aren't working together."

"Ugh." Steele squirmed away and stood up. "That's enough mushy gushy for now. I don't do *feelings*."

Aria grinned, fully aware that Steele was a lot more

emotional than she let on. "Whatever, crazy. Help me pick out an outfit and look for the wrap party tonight."

"Now *that* I can do." Steele was already pulling clothes apart on the rack to one side of the room. "Let's go slutty tonight."

"I'm not going slutty," Aria countered, thinking of Russ's attendance.

Steele sighed. "You always turn down slutty. What about half slutty?"

"What's half slutty?"

Steele held up a dress that had no cleavage. It completely covered her chest and wrapped her neck, leaving only her arms and shoulders bare.

Aria frowned. "How is that half slutty?"

Steele held it up against her body and indicated the hem at the bottom. It barely touched the top of her thighs.

Laughing, Aria shook her head. "So, I'm a nun on top and then naked on the bottom?"

"Exactly. Half slutty."

Aria took the dress and held it up to her own body. It went a little lower on her because she was shorter than Steele, reaching about mid-thigh. "Pair these with knee-high boots to cover my legs and I'll wear it."

Steele pumped her fist through the air. "Finally! Maybe you'll meet a guy tonight."

"I am *not* dating right now," Aria countered, closing the dressing room door so she could get changed. "Not even interested."

"Imagine how pissed Russ would be if he saw you with another guy though." Steele handed her a set of suede boots that matched the emerald green cocktail dress perfectly. "It's the perfect revenge for his cheating ass."

Not many people knew about her affair with Russ, but

Steele was part of her inner circle. Still, she had no desire to make Russell jealous. She just wanted him gone.

"I think I've learned my lesson about dating people I work with," Aria countered, lifting her shirt over her head and tossing it onto the couch. "And there's no one here I'd want to date anyway."

Steele shrugged. She was lining makeup on the counter. "There was a new guy on set today. Sexy as hell in that suit. I might have to call dibs on that."

"You're engaged," Aria reminded her. She had to admit though, Steele was right. Shepherd Film's new CEO was handsome as hell. So handsome, in fact, that she'd already completely blanked on his name from when he introduced himself. His smoldering blue eyes, rugged jaw, and broad shoulders had completely eclipsed her attention for a moment.

Steele winked at her in her reflection in the mirror as she stood behind Aria and zipped up the back of the dress. "Engaged, not blind. Sit. I'm going to do a smoky eye tonight."

"Like you'd ever leave Xavier. I've never seen two people more in love." Aria grabbed Steele's phone off the counter, clicking it on to show her the background photo. It was of Steele and a tattooed man kissing, arms wrapped around each other.

Steele blushed and took her phone back. "It's true. We're really fucking cute." Aria sat still as Steele began wiping off the makeup from filming. "And I'm about to make you really fucking cute, so you better not waste it on another night alone with your battery-operated boyfriend."

She giggled, feeling her face flush with heat. "Steele!"

Part of her had to admit, she wasn't as closed off to dating and men as she let on. She was focused on her career and not about to let a man get in the way of that, but it would be really nice to have someone to fall asleep next to again.

The truth was, Aria was lonely, and she was starting to think it was time to do something about that.

Keep Reading Nudes!

booksbysarahrobinson.com/books/nudes

EXCERPT FROM MISADVENTURES IN THE CAGE

A MISADVENTURES ROMANCE

CHAPTER ONE

"Oh my God...Josie? Josie Gray?" A young African American woman with short black hair and a vibrantly metallic dress on sidled up to her at the bar. "Can I please get a picture with you?"

Josie shot back the glass of tequila and then sucked on the lime, hissing as it hit her stomach hard. She was already four shots in and each one was helping her forget the giant rejection letter she was carrying around in her purse.

We regret to inform you that the position of sous chef is no longer available blah blah blah.

She got the point. She was never going to be a chef. Every job application she'd sent in over the last year had been turned down.

Not that she was even allowed to be one anyway.

"Sure," she replied, finally turning to the woman and putting on her best fake smile.

The woman held up her iPhone, turning the camera around to face them and put on her best duck face as she posed for the camera next to Josie.

Josie just smiled and then turned back to the bar as soon as the photo was done.

"Another one," she indicated to the bartender, but when she lifted her hand to motion, she knocked over her glass. Thankfully, it didn't shatter, but it made a loud ass noise as it clattered against the bar.

The bartender shook his head, casting her a pitying look. God, she hated that. "Miss Gray, I think you've had enough. Why don't I call you a cab?"

"No," she sighed loudly. Admittedly, she was getting tired and had probably had enough. Plus, she couldn't really afford TMZ to find her and write an article about how the reality television star was wasted and falling all over herself at a local bar. Hell, it was the entire reason she'd come to this place off the strip to begin with—anonymity. So much for that. "I'll order a Lyft. Thank you, though."

She paid her check and then pulled out her phone, ordering a ride through the ride share app. Honestly, she wasn't normally like this. She didn't regularly go get drunk by herself at a bar off the Las Vegas strip in a seedy part of town.

Hell, this entire town was a seedy part of town depending on how you looked at it.

She'd spent her entire life living in Las Vegas though, so it was home to her. She was comfortable with its antics and qualms. Something about it...she could handle. At least, that's what she told herself.

Pulling her sweater up around her shoulders, she grabbed her purse and decided to wait for her Lyft out front. She could really use the still, night air to sober up before getting in a lurching car ride. God forbid she puke in the back of someone else's car.

She debated canceling the Lyft and just calling her

driver, but then he would tell her brother where she'd been and she'd never hear the end of it. No, she needed the time off the clock and away from the freaking cameras.

"Hey, Miss," a voice called out to her as she stood on the front steps of the bar trying to take some deep breaths. "You left this on the bar."

She turned to see an older gentleman, maybe twenty years her senior, approaching her. He was holding a tube of lipstick. She didn't recognize it and it certainly wasn't hers. She never wore lipstick.

She shook her head. "That's not mine."

"Are you sure?" He frowned, then glanced back up at her. "I bet it would look real pretty on your chocolate skin."

Josie pulled her sweater tighter around her, hoping the Lyft decided to show up sooner rather than later. "It's not mine," she repeated.

"Why don't you try it on?" he insisted. "Let's just test it out."

"No." She moved away from him, but he approached her faster.

"Just try it on, sweet thing." He grabbed her wrist and twisted it, yanking her backward. "I just want to see how it looks on ya."

"Let go of me!" she yelled, struggling to free her arm from his grasps.

"Don't be such an uppity little bitch," the older man said, squeezing her wrist tighter and tighter until she cried out in pain. "I've seen you on TV before."

"Hey!" A fist came out of nowhere and landed squarely against the older man's jaw.

He staggered back, releasing Josie's wrist and clutching his bruising face. "What the hell?"

"The lady said let go," the owner of the fist—a tall, buff

young man who looked like a brick wall stuffed in a suit—instructed her attacker. "I suggest you listen to women when they talk. I'd also suggest you leave and not come back. Now."

The older man scurried away like a dog with his tail between his legs. She wasn't sorry to see him go.

The newcomer turned back to her, concern etched on his features as his brows furrowed. "Are you okay?"

"I...I think so?" She got back up to her feet and examined her wrist, wincing at the pain.

He noticed her expression right away. "We need to get you to a hospital."

"No way," she opposed the idea right away. "I'm not spending all night in a hospital room when I know it's not broken. It just needs some ice probably."

Plus, she couldn't afford the fall out from the media over yet another family scandal. It was bad enough that her entire family was on a reality television show thanks to her brother's career that chronicled her every move, but knowing that any little thing she did could be used as fodder for an episode was a nightmare waiting to happen.

"See, I can still move it?" She gingerly moved her wrist.

A small smirk played across his lips and she couldn't help but notice a slight Irish accent to his words. "Useful."

"Thank you for your help," she stammered, trying to find something to say to this incredibly gorgeous man who'd just rode in like Prince Charming and saved her life. "I'll just go find my Lyft now."

"What's your name?" he asked, seeming to ignore everything she just said.

"Josie." It was a nice change of pace to run into someone who didn't know who she was. Although, that wasn't very unusual with men because they weren't really the target demographic for her family's show.

He nodded. "I'm Callan."

"Nice to meet you, Callan." She started to walk away again, but he interrupted her again.

"Need a ride home?" he asked, motioning to his car parked against the curb. Of course, it had to be a freaking Range Rover. She wondered who the hell was this guy. It certainly wasn't unusual in Las Vegas to run in to celebrities, but she didn't recognize him...although something about his face...he did look familiar.

She glanced down at her phone and checked her Lyft app. Her driver was still thirteen minutes away. *What the hell?* She canceled the ride. "Sure? Why not."

A ride with a life-saving, potential celebrity sounded safer anyway than with a total stranger vetted only by an app. At least, that's the story she was going to tell herself to convince herself to get into the car with this drop dead handsome man. And when she said drop dead handsome, she meant it. The dude was gawking-worthy. Chiseled muscles on every inch of his body that she could see. Long, brown wavy hair tied back in a pony tail, and blue eyes that made her knees feel like they were made of jello.

"Is this your car?" she asked, motioning to the Range Rover.

He nodded and opened the passenger door for her. "Hop in."

"Hold on. One second." She walked around to the front of the car and took a picture of the car and license plate and sent it off in a quick text to her best friend, Emily.

"Did you just take a picture of my license plate?" he asked, one brow raised as he watched her.

"And texted it to my friend," she confirmed, waltzing past him and climbing into the passenger seat of the car.

He chuckled, leaning against the door frame. "Can I ask why?"

"In case you murder me, obviously." She turned to face him, giving him a deadpan expression like it was the most obvious thing ever. Honestly, it was. Her mother had taught her that trick years ago, and you learn a thing or two growing up in Las Vegas. Men are a lot less likely to act nefariously when they know they're being held accountable by an anonymous third party.

A grin spread wide across his face and it only made his beautiful features all the more glorious. "Smart lady." He closed her car door and she watched as he walked around the car and then climbed into the driver's seat. "Where to, Ms. Precaution?"

Maybe it was the tequila talking, or maybe it was the fact that he was daring her to throw caution to the wind, or maybe she was just fed up with the monotony of her life and wanted to throw a wrench at things. She wasn't sure what made the next words come out of her mouth. All she knew was that she said them and she didn't want to take them back...and thank God, she didn't.

"Take me to your place."

Live on All Retailers:

booksbysarahrobinson.com/books/misadventures-in-the-cage/

ABOUT THE AUTHOR

Sarah Robinson first started her writing career as a published poet in high school, and then continued in college, winning several poetry awards and being published in multiple local literary journals.

Never expecting to make a career of it, a freelance writing Craigslist job accidentally introduced her to the world of book publishing. Lengthening her writing from poetry to novels, Robinson published her first book through a small press publisher, before moving into self-publishing, and then finally accepting a contract from Penguin Random House two years later. She continues to publish both traditionally and indie with over 18+ novels to her name with publishers like Penguin, Waterhouse Press, Hachette, and more. She has achieved awards and accolades including 2021 Vivian Award Finalist, Top 10 iBooks Bestseller, Top

25 Amazon Kindle Bestseller, and Top 5 Barnes & Noble
Bestseller. She has been published in three languages.

In her personal life, Sarah Robinson is happily married to
the gentle giant of her dreams and the duo recently
welcomed to the world their first baby, Norah Grace. They
have a home full of love, snuggly pets, and are happily living
in Arlington, Virginia.

Follow the Author on Social Media

booksbysarahrobinson.com
subscribepage.com/sarahrobinsonnewsletter
facebook.com/booksbysarahrobinson
twitter.com/booksby_sarah
goodreads.com/booksbysarahrobinson
instagram.com/booksbysarahrobinson

SHEER

At the Mall Series

(*Romantic Comedy Shorts*)

Mall I Want for Christmas is You

Mall You Need is Love

Mall Out of Luck

Heart Lake Series

(*Small Town Romances*)

Dreaming of a Heart Lake Christmas

Standalone Novels

Not a Hero: A Bad Boy Marine Romance

Misadventures in the Cage

One Night Stand Serial

Second Shot of Whiskey

Women's Fiction

Every Last Drop